The
DOCTOR
And
The
ENTERPRISE

By Jean Airey
with illustrations by Mahlon Fawce
and Tom Holtkamp

PIONEER BOOKS, INC.   LAS VEGAS

Library of Congress Cataloging-in-Publication Data
Airey, Jean
      The Doctor and the Enterprise

      1. Television I. Title
ISBN #1-55698-218-6

International Standard Book Number: #1-55698-218-6

First Printing 1989

chapter one

The alien sound seemed to pierce The Captain's ears. He stopped, alone in the corridor, trying to pinpoint its origin.

The transporter room.

He turned and ran towards the door as the klaxon alarm of Red Alert sounded. Damn! he thought. It seemed that the Enterprise could not even make the final trip back to Earth after completing her five-year mission without complications. First an emergency rescue of a Cultural Survey and Contact team and the crew of the liner that had been transporting them, then a freak magnetic storm that had buffeted the ship unmercifully and taken out the subspace radio, and now...

As he entered the room, The Lieutenant was staring at a large boxlike structure that stood on several of the transporter pads. It was about eight feet tall with small opaqued windows at the top, a white light on the roof that was rotating slowly and lettering above the windows that said `POLICE PUBLIC CALL BOX'.

"Report, Lieutenant."

"It just appeared, sir."

"The transporter wasn't activated?"

"No, sir. We were performing signaling tests, but it was not activated."

The door at the front of the box started to open. Both The Captain and The Lieutenant had their lasers out as a man emerged.

Over six feet tall, he was wearing a heavy coat over clothing that reminded The Captain of the earth styles of the 1890s. A long scarf was wrapped around his neck, hanging down in front on both sides to the floor. A floppy hat partially covered an abundance of brown curly hair. His blue eyes seemed to focus suddenly on The Captain and The Lieutenant. One cheek looked

bruised, and he swayed slightly.

"Oh bother," he said with a decided British accent, "this isn't London."

"Just stand there and keep your hands where we can see them," The Captain said. He did not seem to be a menace, but The Captain had seen his ship threatened too often to take any chances.

"No need to panic." The man raised his hands slowly and eyed the lasers as if he recognized them.

The door behind The Captain opened, and two security guards took positions on the right and left while The Physician and The Scientist came over to The Captain.

"Captain?" The Scientist already had his tricorder going.

"The box materialized in that position — and he—" The Captain motioned with his head to the stranger who was watching the proceedings with curiosity, "came out of it. He hasn't made any hostile moves. Oh, Scientist, the transporter wasn't activated."

The stranger eyed the assembly as if he were accustomed to weighing the odds against him. The Captain did not miss that look. In spite of the stranger's unimpressive appearance, he felt uneasy. He could hear the combined tricorders of The Scientist and The Physician humming behind him.

"Scientist?"

"The — box — would seem to be a representation of a middle twentieth century English Police Call Box. However, there are some anomalies...".

"He's not human, Cap." The Physician interrupted.

"Captain," said The Scientist, "I am getting some unusual readings from inside the device."

As The Captain was realizing that the "box" had now become a "device", the stranger moved quickly towards its door. The security guards fired instantly, but he still managed to close the door as he fell, collapsing on the transporter step.

"Lieutenant, see if you can get that door open. Scientist, is he armed?"

The Lieutenant moved up to the door of the device, but the door would not open. The Scientist was carefully analyzing his tricorder readings. "Captain, the pockets of his coat are filled with a great many objects. I am unable to ascertain if any of these might be some type of weapon."

"Empty his pockets." The Captain ordered one of the security guards.

"Captain, in view of the quantity of items present, it might be more expedient to remove the garment." The Captain nodded and the security guards moved to comply. As the security guards were removing the coat and jacket, one of them let the unconscious body slip slightly. The Scientist caught the head just before it hit the floor again.

He stiffened suddenly as the contact was made, his head snapping up and his eyes abruptly glazing. It took a moment before The Captain realized that somehow, without willing it, The Scientist had joined minds with the alien.

"Scientist!" The Captain moved quickly and tore The Scientist's hands from their grip, letting the alien's head fall back to the floor. "Are you all right?"

The Scientist's eyes remained glazed for a second and then he responded, "Quite all right, Captain."

"What happened?"

"He has — unusual — psychic abilities. Unconscious — I unwittingly established the mind-meld."

"What did you find out?"

The Scientist looked at The Captain reproachfully. "Captain, the mind-meld was made accidently." The Captain realized that The Scientist had in some way violated his sense of ethics by entering the meld, and now The Captain was compounding the situation by asking questions.

"Does he present a danger to the ship?" Surely The Scientist could at least answer that.

"No, Captain, he does not." The Scientist seemed to have retreated behind the thickest wall of Ozian reserve.

"Fizz, what is he?"

"Nothing I've ever seen or heard of before." The Physician moved closer to the unconscious body, clad now in a white shirt, vest, pants, boots and with the long, multicolored scarf still wrapped around its neck. "He has a double circulatory system — not like The Scientist's — literally two hearts, one on each side of his chest, some kind of a double breathing system, body temperature 17 degrees, blood pressure almost nonexistent. I can't tell you what he is, Jim, but even his response to the laser fire was abnormal — he was still conscious as he fell. As a matter of fact, I believe he may have sustained some type of head injury." The Physician ran the medical tricorder over the stranger's head again. "He did — but it looks like it's an aggravation of a recent previous injury. And that's unusual — his skull is very thick, so what could have caused the original injury...?"

"How long will he remain unconscious?"

"Jim, I can't say — longer than normal, with a combination of two laser stuns and at the very least a severe concussion."

"Doctor," said The Scientist, "your ability as a prognostician would seem to leave something to be desired."

The Captain and The Physician looked at the stranger. His eyes were open, and he was very apparently conscious.

"Gentlemen," he said, eyeing the security guards as they moved back into their "alert" position. "Don't you think that some two sided conversation might be more informative than your one sided version?" He smiled, as if finding their reactions deeply funny.

The Captain noticed with surprise that the security guards were relaxing. "Do you feel well enough to talk to us?"

"Yes, of course. I love to talk — if you are willing to talk and not shoot. I really hate stun guns."

Glancing at The Physician and The Scientist and receiving an answering shrug of shoulders and a tilted eyebrow, The Captain turned back to the stranger and said, "We can talk in one of our briefing rooms." The stranger got up slowly, accepting The Physician's help. "Lieutenant," said The Captain, "come with us. Scientist, have you been able to clear up that subspace communication problem yet?"

"No, Captain, the fault is not in the computer scanning system. The Communications Officer and The Engineer are continuing to work on it."

"I want to be informed as soon as anything is found out about what caused it — and I want it fixed."

"Yes, sir." The Scientist turned to relay the order to the bridge, informing them that the Captain could be reached in briefing room 4 at the Teleporter level.

The security guards moved to either side of the man. He glanced at them and then over to The Captain. "Do you consider me so dangerous?"

"I have seen danger come to my ship in many forms — I prefer not to take chances." In spite of The Scientist's statement, The Captain was not ready to relax his guard. Their eyes locked, and the stranger smiled in amusement again. The Captain's eyes narrowed and then, suddenly returning the smile, he motioned the guards away. "Lieutenant, keep your laser ready."

"A compromise — a very judicious choice."

"What is your name?" asked The Captain.

"Oh, I'm the Doctor."

"The Doctor?" echoed The Captain as the group left the room.

"Doctor who?" asked The Physician.

"That's right," said The Doctor, beaming at The Physician. The Physician looked baffled.

"Doctor," said The Scientist. "I believe that the 'name' was 'The Doctor' — and I should assume that it is in the nature of a title, and can be most appropriately used without any surname. However, The Doctor apparently is accustomed to the human desire to attach at least two names to all sentient beings. If you wish to use a duonomen form of address, he would not object if you refer to him as Doctor Who."

The Doctor had been listening to The Scientist with an infectious smile impossibly growing on his face and The Captain began smiling too. Somehow an individual who could appreciate The Scientist at his most precise did not seem to be a threat to the Enterprise.

They went into the briefing room and sat down. The Doctor was looking at The Scientist closely.

"You're not human either?"

"I am a Wizard."

"Wizard? From a planet called Oz?"

An eyebrow raised. "Yes. Do you know it?"

"From somewhere — I'll think of it."

"Well, Doctor," said The Captain, "you must realize that the first question that we need answered is, What are you doing here?"

"I don't know." The Doctor grinned as The Captain winced.

"You mean that you did not control the method of your arrival on this ship?" asked The Scientist.

"Exactly. I was expecting to return to London — in June of 1980, and instead materialized here."

"Did you use the device in the Transporter room?"

"Yes. Ever since I've been using her she doesn't always go where I expect her to — and I can certainly assure you that I was not expecting to arrive on your ship."

"What planet are you from originally?" asked The Captain, hoping to get a simple answer that might help solve the mystery.

"Narnia."

"Scientist?" The Captain had never heard of it, but that did not mean that it did not exist.

"No record of any planet by that name." The Scientist looked up from the science computer viewer.

The Doctor was studying The Scientist intently. Under his breath, The Captain could hear him mutter "Moz, Coz, Boz, Oz!" He turned to The Captain suddenly.

"What year is this — Earth time — say, since 1980?"

"224 years."

The Doctor looked puzzled. "Captain, it would seem that we both have something of an enigma on our hands. You have me, and I have a Wizard surviving centuries after his race — and his planet — was utterly destroyed in a massive civil war." The Scientist turned and stared at him.

"Parallel Universes," said The Captain.

"You are familiar with the theory?"

"I — we — have experienced the phenomenon before."

"Can you give me the coordinates of your planet?" The Scientist asked.

The Doctor could. The Scientist entered them into the computer and looked at the response with resignation. "That planetary system was destroyed when its sun became a red giant 140,000 years ago."

"So my people do not exist in your universe."

"It would seem unlikely. There are very few intelligent, space-travelling races that are completely unknown, and The Physician has no record of any race of your type. What do you call yourselves?"

"Time Lords."

The Scientist's eyebrow raised, but The Captain decided to interrupt before his first officer's curiosity could be indulged further. "It would seem that what we need to do is to find out how to return you to your own universe."

"No, Captain, I think that the first thing we must find out is whose universe we are in now."

The intercom beeped. "Bridge to The Captain."

"The Captain here."

"Helmsman here, Captain. We've got what appears to be a large group of ships just within scanner range."

"Is the subspace radio fixed?"

"No, sir. We have not been able to obtain any transmissions on any standard Starfleet frequencies."

"I'll be right up."

The Captain turned to The Doctor who had been listening to the conversation with a curious mixture of interest and amusement. "Doctor, would you care to join us? This might prove to be the answer to your question."

"I'd be delighted."

The Physician scowled. "Cap, I don't think that The Doctor should be moving around too much until I can tell—"

"Oh, I'm quite all right — really. I've almost gotten used to being stunned by something or another." The Doctor smiled at The Physician.

"I would suggest that, given the circumstances, The Doctor's presence on the bridge could prove of some benefit." The Scientist interjected.

"Very well, then, The Doctor will join us. Lieutenant, record your report on this and then you're off duty. I want all other transporter personnel alerted in case we acquire any other visitors."

On their way to the bridge, The Captain noticed that The Doctor took in the usual sights and sounds of the starship with interest but without amazement. He seemed to note with somewhat increased interest the presence of two Munchkins— commenting to The Scientist —"So you have alien species in the crew." The Scientist did not seem to think that the remark was worthy of response, but The Captain observed that The Doctor found The Scientist's lack of response an apparent cause for thought. His only other comment came when they got into the turbolift system and The Captain said "Bridge" causing the turbolift to begin its usual forward and upward motion.

"Voice controlled?"

The Captain nodded.

"How convenient."

"We find it so," said The Scientist.

"A logical approach?" said The Doctor, smiling at The Scientist and, surprisingly, winking at The Captain. The Scientist did not respond, which seemed to afford The Doctor more amusement. The Captain began to wonder if The Doctor pictured himself as some sort of intergalactic comedian.

The door opened on the bridge and The Captain moved to the navigational console.

"How close are those ships?"

"I can pick them up on visual scanning now, sir," said The Helmsman, adjusting the controls.

"Put it on the screen — highest magnification."

"Yes, sir."

A swarm of small ships came into view. Globe-like, they seemed to fill the viewscreen like dozens of small stars. The Captain heard The Doctor take a deep breath. "Identification?"

The Scientist was checking the readings at the Science Station. "Type of ship unknown to our computers, some type of alien lifeform within — also unknown."

"Captain," said The Doctor, stepping down beside The Captain. "It's my universe, and I would suggest that you move away from those ships as rapidly as possible."

All traces of the comedian had left. "Why?" The Captain asked.

"They're Teamsters—freight and shipping vessels from the look of them and the number, but they usually have some armed escorts." He glanced around the Bridge, taking in the assorted personnel, seeming to weigh their experience and the possible reception of what he was saying. Having apparently made some kind of decision, he continued.

"Have you ever met a race whose greatest pleasure was to enslave other people? To conquer, kill, torture and maim — often for the joy it brings them? Who value their own individual lives as nothing — and the lives of other races as less than that?" By now The Doctor was speaking with a seriousness that surprised and impressed The Captain with its deadly concentration. Indeed, The Doctor seemed to have lost the concern for this "audience" and was speaking almost to himself. The Captain glanced around the rest of the Bridge. All of the crew had been listening intently, their attention completely on The Doctor. Even The Communications Officer and The Engineer had crawled out from under the communications panel where they had been working. As The Doctor finished speaking, eyes moved to the viewing screen where the alien vessels were growing larger. That The Doctor was sincere The Captain would not question; that in some situations discretion was the better part of valor he had never doubted.

"We've run into people like that. Scientist — get as much information as you can from the scanners. Helmsman, Moebius six 180 degrees out of here. Communications Officer, Engineer, you can stop working on that radio. Start scanning for any communications on bands outside the Starfleet band, they apparently don't use that high a range here."

The Doctor was smiling again as The Captain finished. "Well, Captain, you and your crew are certainly both quick and efficient." He glanced

around with approval at the organized effort underway on the bridge.

"Doctor," said The Captain, "I think that you and I need to have a talk."

"But of course — at your convenience." The Doctor leaned casually against the bridge rail and smiled at The Captain as though he were in complete control of an ordinary situation.

With a feeling of exasperation, The Captain turned to The Scientist. "Have you been...?" He heard a crash behind him and as he turned around saw that The Doctor had collapsed and The Physician was bending over him. "Fizz?"

"Cerebrovascular hemorrhage — we'd better get him down to sickbay."

"Go ahead."

The Physician was calling for the sickbay team when The Scientist turned to The Captain.

"Captain, armed vessels from that fleet were attempting to pursue us. We have outdistanced them. However, long range scanners indicate similar vessels throughout this area."

"How long can we maintain evasive action?"

"Difficult to say, Captain. We have no familiarity with these ships or their capabilities. If this is indeed a parallel universe, we cannot even determine with certainly where we could go in relative safety until we can effect our return."

"In other words, we need The Doctor."

"If he does possess the knowledge he claims, and if he is willing to assist us — then yes, we need him."

The sickbay team was removing their patient. The Captain looked at the unconscious form.

"Helmsman, you have the con. Keep us clear of any involvement with anything. The Scientist and I'll be in sickbay. If I can get any more information from The Doctor, I'll tell you."

Down in sickbay, The Physician scowled at the indicators over the bed where The Doctor lay.

"How bad is it?" asked The Captain, concerned that the only source of information about this alternate universe would be unavailable to them.

"Cap, I don't know what normal is for him — so I can't tell how badly the hemorrhaging is effecting him — except that he is unconscious, and I would say that if the injury is doing that then it's very bad indeed. There seem to be previously damaged areas in that part of the brain, and while he also seems to have a remarkable healing ability, what's happening now is more than his body mechanism can handle on its own."

"What are you going to do?"

"I suspect that, even with the damage, given time, he could recover without my doing anything."

"Fizz, we don't have time." The Physician still looked unconvinced and The Captain continued his argument. "He is the only clue we have to where we are and possibly how we got here — and how we can get back in one piece. I need him conscious — and well — as soon as possible."

"Cap, there's a large blood clot between his skull and his brain. It covers quite a large area and there is active bleeding from inside the brain to that area. The clot has to come out and the bleeding stopped."

"You've treated our crew for that kind of thing before."

"I've been able to treat them medically. I know what medications I can use on our people — even The Scientist — mostly. I wouldn't dare use any of them on him. I have absolutely no way of determining what the possible side effects would be. The only possible thing I could do would be to operate and surgically remove the clot and cauterize the bleeding."

"Then you'll have to do that."

"Without anesthesia? I've got the same problem with what we normally use for pain killers. Damn it, Cap, you saw that even the lasers didn't have the normal effect on him. If I use a drug, I could kill him. If I don't use one — Cap, I'm a doctor, not a butcher."

"Doctor?"

The Physician turned. The Doctor's eyes were open but were still slightly glazed. He looked at The Physician. "What's the problem?"

The Physician explained.

"Normally I could tell you what would be effective — but I don't think I'm up to that. I have been trying to get into a catatonic trance — which would enable you to operate humanely, but I suspect the area involved..."

The Physician nodded. "It would interfere with your ability to do that."

The Captain noticed that The Doctor's speech had become slightly blurred. It was obviously an effort for him to talk, and the pain indicator was rising higher with each effort.

"You are proposing a manual procedure."

The Physician nodded.

"That would seem to be the acceptable alternative."

"There is a possibility that you will not be unconscious during the operation."

"I quite understand that — but from what I saw out there — we have little time to spare."

The Physician still looked reluctant.

"Come now," he snapped impatiently, "surely you are as skillful as your own Incan physicians. The operation must be done. I would suggest that you strap...". He slipped into unconsciousness again.

"Okay, Cap, we'll try it. Only pray that he stays unconscious."

"I though the brain had no nerve endings," The Captain said.

"Yours doesn't," The Physician said grimly.

With the restraints in place and The Doctor turned on one side to expose the area for the operation, a sterile field was established and The Physician began the delicate operation.

The Doctor did not stay unconscious. As The Physician finished opening the skull, his eyes opened again. The Captain saw his hands move against the restraints. Suddenly The Scientist moved over and took them. The eyes of the two aliens met and something was exchanged between them.

"Sometimes it helps to have someone to hold on to." Did The Captain really hear that?

Almost an answering smile came as The Doctor's eyes closed again. But The Captain saw the pressure of the hands grasping The Scientist's and knew that the man remained aware of The Physician suctioning out the area. Only when the laser cauterizer was used did the hands relax again and full unconsciousness return.

"That seems to be it. Nurse, were you able to make a repair patch from those skull fragments?"

"Yes, Doctor."

The Physician carefully molded the "patch" into place. Only a small area of bone had been removed and the patch, made from the patient's own tissue and bone, would rapidly fuse the open area with as much protection as the original. "Cap, I think we did it." The Physician looked at the indicators carefully. "Pain is down, both hearts in sinus rhythm, blood pressure stable, alpha rhythm flowing. Was he conscious at all?"

"Yes."

"Damn. I still feel like a butcher having to operate like that."

"Not at all, Doctor," came the voice from the bed. "It was a very well done job and I thank you." The Doctor looked as though he was going to get up as soon as The Nurse finished removing the restraints.

"You stay right there," barked The Physician.

"But Physician," The Doctor said in an injured tone, "I feel very well now and there are things...".

"Don't tell me how you feel. You're staying there for at least another 24 hours — and if I have to keep the restraints on you, I will."

The Doctor's gaze and The Physician's clashed. The Doctor raised himself to a half-sitting position and The Physician moved forward. The Captain looked at the indicators; they were starting to move again. The Scientist stepped between The Doctor and The Physician. "Doctor, I would suggest that you follow The Physician's prescription. I do not think that the time need be wasted. We can provide you with a tie-in to the library computer from here. If you are going to help us, you will need to know quite a bit more about us." The Physician glared at The Scientist.

"Fizz," The Captain said, "you know that he isn't just going to lie there."

"Very well," The Physician turned back to his patient. "But you're not to get up."

"Agreed — Fizz," and traces of the old smile appeared as The Doctor lay back. The Scientist started toward the door. "Oh, and Scientist," The Scientist turned back and looked at The Doctor questioningly. "Thank you. I have not often come upon a gesture made as appropriately and as willingly." Without waiting for a reply The Doctor turned and smiled at The Nurse. "Do you have a listing...".

"Nurse," The Physician interrupted. "I want the biolab to do a full analysis on him. And Doctor, before you start playing around with the computer, you tell The Nurse all about your medical history. If you're going to be around here I want to know how to treat you."

For a moment The Captain thought that The Scientist was going to make another remark, but he turned and went out the door.

"Fizz," from the grin on The Doctor's face, The Captain suspected that he was about to say something that would provoke a reaction from The Physician. "Do you rally think it essential to have all my medical history? I'm 749 years old, and as charming as The Nurse is, that might take more time...".

"If you could restrain yourself to the pertinent facts, I think that the time will be sufficient. I'm sure that in 749 years you've learned to restrain yourself when it's necessary."

Score one for The Physician, thought The Captain.

"And in the next 24 hours, I expect you to rest — or sleep — or whatever you do — for at least eight," The Physician continued.

The Doctor looked quizzical and The Physician paused.

"Six?"

No response.

"Four?"

"Four hours should be sufficient. At the end of my stay here, Captain, I would suggest that you and I and your chief officers get together."

The Captain had an uneasy feeling that the control of the ship had been transferred, but reminded himself that The Doctor was only expressing what he himself had already decided. "As soon as The Physician says you're fit, I'll call the meeting."

The Captain and The Physician walked toward the sickbay door. "What was that last part to The Scientist about, Cap?"

"If The Doctor travels around alone — as he would seem to — he must often find himself fighting on his own in unpleasant situations. How old did he say he was?"

"749."

"The Scientist should find that...".

"Fascinating!"

As The Captain entered the Bridge, The Scientist got up from the command chair.

"Report, Scientist?"

"We seem to have outdistanced the Sontaran fleet. However, scanners indicate considerable activity in most of this area of space. We have been following a path which would seem to lead to an area of comparative inactivity. When the Doctor recovers—"

"We can expect The Doctor to be available to us in 24 hours. Until then, we will simply have to avoid making any sort of contact with the ships and people in this universe."

"Captain," said The Communications Officer, "I am now able to receive transmissions from vessels in the area. We are unable to translate them coherently, however."

"Very well, Lieutenant. Let me know as soon as possible when we can tell what they're talking about. I want all senior officers in briefing room 2 in one hour."

"Yes, sir." The Communications Officer turned back to her communications panel.

Inside the briefing room, The Captain looked around at the officers already gathered. The Physician was late, and they were waiting for him.

For five years I've been with this crew through all sorts of adventures — bizarre and commonplace, he thought. I've lost 92 crewmen, and for all my command experience, I'll never accept those deaths as being necessary. This ship and its crew are my life, and whatever it takes, I'll see that they get back to their own universe. It's part of my mission, my responsibility. No glory in doing that; it's part of the job. And when it's completed? He decided not to try to guess what Starfleet would do then. Anyway, The Physician had arrived and they could get working on the current problem.

"Sorry I'm late, Cap," The Physician said as he came in and sat down at the briefing table. "I finally managed to get my patient settled."

"Was there much of a problem?"

"Not much more than I'm used to," The Physician looked at The Captain and The Scientist accusingly. "Although I must say that you two don't generally involve The Nurse with fantastic tales of wild adventures, persuade the Medical staff — and all my other patients to join in a feast of jellybabies...".

"Jellybabies?" asked The Captain.

"Some kind of candy about two centimeters long, shaped like a swaddled infant, and they come in assorted flavors. He seems to have an infinite supply and he's got everyone in sickbay munching on them. In between passing out candy and talking to Chris, he's been running through the data on the library computer — at fast speed. I finally had to tell him that I'd put him in isolation with no computer before he agreed to rest."

"Will he be able to talk to us tomorrow?"

"Yes. Although if he disrupts my sickbay much more, I might let you have him earlier."

"If I might make a suggestion, Captain," The Scientist said.

"I think that both The Physician and I would welcome it, Scientist."

"When we rescued the passengers and crew of the liner Crotone, there was a Cultural Survey and Contact team on board." The Captain nodded. CS&C was a recently created specialized division in Starfleet. They had their own chain of command, but while on his ship they were under him. Since the rescue, they had been quite helpful in keeping the Crotone crew and passengers out of his own crew's way. The addition of some 250 "passengers" stretched the Enterprise's normal resources to an uncomfortable limit.

"Do you think they can help us, Scientist?"

"The Lieutenant who is in charge of the team has an exemplary record in initial survey expeditions and on this last expedition has been credited by the other members of the team with enabling them to be retrieved by the Crotone after their Captain was killed. Since we have a member of a new culture on board, it would seem logical to assign her to 'study' him."

"What's her background, Scientist?" The Physician asked.

"She has a PhD in Xenobiology and is also a certified paramedical technician."

27

"Well, I'd certainly be glad to have her assigned to him." The Physician said. "What's her name?"

"Stephans, Lt. Dorcy Stephans," The Captain answered. "As soon as we're through here, I'll notify her of her new assignment."

The Physician nodded with relief. "The sooner the better."

"Now, if we could come to the main concern of this meeting. Engineer, what is the current damage report?"

"We had some minor problems immediately after that storm, mostly caused by the vibration. They've all been checked and cleared. But there seems to be something going off balance in the matter-antimatter mix when we're at Moebius speed. As long as we stay at Moebius speed, I can't try to clear it up."

"You want to go to impulse power?"

"Aye, Captain."

"Scientist, is there any sign of an enemy vessel in scanning range?"

"Negative, Captain. We are presently in an area of space which shows no signs of any lifeform activity."

"Very well. Engineer, cut back to impulse power, but remember that we could have to cut in Moebius drive on short notice."

"Aye. We'll leave an emergency cut-in — but we still won't be able to tolerate high Moebius speed until we find the main trouble."

"Captain," The Scientist said, "we have a problem with the computer control to engineering life support."

"I thought that was all in a separate system with full emergency backup? Wasn't that what we just had installed?"

"We now have an independent primary control and a secondary control which is a complete duplicate of the first. We also have a tertiary system which can provide up to two hours of full support. During the storm, the ROMs on the primary control were erased. It will take 35 hours to reprogram and reinstall them on the primary system."

"Then we're running on the secondary system with the tertiary as the backup."

"Exactly. However, if something happens to the secondary system, and the tertiary system exceeds its life span, a failsafe back to the main computer will start a half-hour countdown to destruct the ship."

chapter two

"Now whose bright idea was that?" The Physician asked.

"It's supposed to force an organized abandonment of the ship's crew to the nearest M-type planet — with a rescue robot beacon detached, and no chance of the ship falling into the 'Wrong hands'." The Captain smiled at The Physician. "Starfleet is apparently discouraging heroics."

"But Captain, we don't even have enough spacesuits or evacuation equipment for everyone now — with the people from the Crotone on board." The Physician said in concern.

"And there are no M-type planets within transporter range," The Scientist added.

"And what good would a robot beacon do us here?" The Physician continued.

"Gentlemen, aren't we looking at the worst possible circumstances?" The Captain said. "In 34 hours we'll have the primary system back up. By that time The Engineer will have us underway at full Moebius power, and in only 24 hours the Doctor will be able to at least guide us around this universe in safety. We should have ample time to figure out how to get back to our own universe. All we have to do is stay out of trouble for a very short while."

"Aye, Captain," The Engineer said, "it would be a mighty strange set of circumstances that would get us into trouble again that quick." He stopped and thought for a moment. "But Captain, do you really think that we can trust the Doctor?"

"What do you think?"

"Well, he's an alien. His travelling device is of a type we've never heard of. We dinna know anything about him — but he seemed to assume that we'd both be on the same side against a bunch of people like the Evil Witches. He seems to have

had considerable experience in dealin' with humans — but we dinna know how he go it."

"What makes you assume that he has had such extensive contact with humans?" The Scientist asked.

"Well, Scientist, it might not be your kind of logic, but it seems to me that anyone who can accept the fact that the natural reaction of a security guard would be to shoot has got to have been around humans for quite a while."

The Captain looked at The Scientist who nodded in agreement. He knew better than to ask The Scientist outright how far he felt the Doctor should be trusted. But he knew enough of his first officer... "We've given him complete access to the library computer. In spite of his disruption of sickbay he seems to be as concerned with our situation as we are."

The Engineer nodded. "It canna be denied that we'll need all the help we can get to get back to our own universe in one piece."

"And if we're going to do that, Engineer, we'd better get to work on what we know we have to do. Meeting dismissed."

As the group got up to leave, The Scientist walked over to The Captain. "Incidentally, Captain, I could not help but notice that at times the Doctor seems to have a very charismatic effect on humans."

"I had noticed that too — but I don't think that it's going to become a problem." The Scientist turned to leave. "Oh Scientist, did you hear how old he is?"

The Scientist turned back, an eyebrow raised. "Indeed, Captain, and have you determined what his total life span would be?"

"No, but...".

"I would venture to say that he is still quite young, measuring his present age against the normal longevity of his race."

The Captain stared at The Scientist's departing back and shook his head in amazement. If The Scientist was right, and the Doctor was still "young", perhaps that explained the seemingly inappropriate burst of humor. Maybe all Time Lords went through this stage before stabilizing into serious adults. At least he did not seem to demonstrate the childlike cruelty that Trelaine had. Somehow The Captain felt that his reasoning might not be completely correct, but it was a comforting thought. All he needed on the ship at this time was a comedian, and an alien one at that.

In the briefing room the next day, The Captain, The Scientist, The Engineer and The Xenobiologist waited for The Physician to arrive with the Doctor. The Physician had reported that The Xenobiologist and the Doctor were working quite well together and that there had been no further major disruptions in sickbay.

"The Captain to bridge."

"The Communications Officer here."

"If you pick up any significant transmissions while we are here, alert me and patch them through."

"Yes, Captain."

The door opened and the Doctor and The Physician entered. The Captain noticed that the Doctor had re-acquired his overcoat, jacket and floppy hat. Well, he thought, with such a low body temperature, the Doctor might well feel cold in the Earth-normal environment of the Enterprise.

"Good morning, everyone," said the Doctor blithely, taking the seat at the table opposite The

Captain. The Captain noticed as he sat down that it was as if the 'head' of the table had suddenly shifted. Well, The Scientist had warned him. Whatever the Doctor had, it was there, it was 'natural', and it affected humans. Wizards too? he wondered.

"Good morning, Doctor. I don't think you've been introduced to The Engineer."

"Chief Engineer," the Doctor responded, rising and offering his hand to The Engineer. Somewhat surprised, The Engineer responded in kind. "And The Xenobiologist and I have been having some fascinating conversations." The Doctor smiled. The Lieutenant smiled. "And of course I am already acquainted with The Scientist and you, Captain." The Doctor glanced over at the Captain quizzically. "Well, Captain, could you fill me in on our present status?"

The Physician snorted. The Captain gathered that the Doctor had not been idle during his confinement in sickbay, even after the disruption had stopped. He probably knew the situation as well as anyone else.

"Scientist?"

"We have been able to successfully avoid all contact with any alien vessels. This is our present position." The computer viewers glowed, indicating the Enterprise and the present star position. "In our universe, this was part of the area controlled by the Klingfree Empire."

"So you don't have much information on it?"

"Very little. Are you familiar with it?"

"Yes, I've been around here before. In this time — in this universe — the Evil Witches are trying to conquer this area from the Rutters."

"Our long range scanners indicate considerable vessel movement."

"Doctor," asked The Captain, "What would happen if we met up with a Sontaran fleet?"

"It would depend on how many of them there were. With your offensive and defensive weapons you could probably escape an attack of, say, twenty to forty of their ships. More than that and they could destroy you." He cocked his head at The Captain.

"Twenty to forty?" queried The Scientist.

"I can't give you a more precise number." The Doctor smiled at The Scientist. "There are a significant number of random factors."

"How large are their fleets?" asked The Engineer.

"It depends on what they're attacking. A massive effort and they think nothing of sending out 400."

The Scientist looked skeptical.

"They don't care how many may be destroyed," the Doctor went on, "they only want to win."

"Don't they value their own pilots and crews?" asked The Captain.

"Oh no. You see, they're clones."

"Clones?"

"Yes. They reproduce by cloning. So any individual life means nothing to them, and they don't think much of races who do respect individual life — especially humans."

The Xenobiologist was frowning. "But cloning would...".

"You must allow for the environmental factors, Lieutenant," interrupted the Doctor, leaning forward on the table. "So many are raised to be leaders, others to follow orders and die."

"Doctor," The Captain said, trying to return the attention of the conversation to the topic he felt to be of primary concern. "You must realize that our primary interest at the moment is to return to our own universe without an entanglement in yours."

"I can certainly sympathize with that." The Doctor leaned back in his chair and put his feet on the table. "If our positions were reversed, I should certainly feel the same way." He grinned.

"And a further consequence of this interest is that we do not want to do anything that might alter the course of events in this universe."

"Ah yes, I have come across that desire to be detached observers before. Your 'Let 'em Be' Directive', I believe you call it." The group nodded. "That might not be so simple." He sat up straight again. "The Evil Witches' scanners have a slightly longer range than yours, and if you have been detected, they will not choose to merely observe you. And Captain, I can also tell you this: you cannot allow your ship to fall into Sontaran hands."

"Possible effect?" asked The Scientist.

"With the knowledge they could gain from the engineering and weaponry of your vessel, you would enable them to conquer the galaxy quite easily." He leaned back again and glanced around the table as if weighing the quality of the people he saw.

"I see," said The Captain.

The Doctor sat suddenly upright. "As a matter of fact you might check the activity in the area surrounding your ship — at the very edge of your scanner range."

"Scientist," snapped The Captain.

"360 degree scanner — alien vessels at the edge of the third sector now."

"Captain," it was The Helmsman. "We have vessels closing in on us from the third sector. The Communications Officer has not been able to complete translation of their transmissions."

"Red Alert, Helmsman. I'm on my way. Well, Doctor, if you're right, it looks as though we'll be fighting our way out of this one." The Captain turned to leave.

"If you take a heading of 185 degrees, Captain, you should be able to get into a relatively safe area," shouted the Doctor as The Captain passed through the door.

On the bridge The Captain found his crew alert and ready for battle. The glow of the red alert light gave an eerie highlight to the area.

"Engineer, do we have Moebius speed?"

"I can give you up to Moebius 2, sir, but beyond that there is still an unstable factor in the matter/anti-matter mix."

"How fast are the Sontaran vessels, Scientist?"

"Presently travelling at Moebius 1, Captain."

"Increase to Moebius 2, Helmsman."

"Aye, Sir."

"The Evil Witches can reach the equivalent of your Moebius 3, Captain." The Captain looked around and saw that the Doctor had seated himself on one of the bridge steps. Wonderful, he thought, now he had a back-seat driver.

"Evil Witches are increasing to Moebius 2 also, Captain." The Scientist studied his science console viewer closely. "Now at Moebius 2.5 and gaining on us."

"Helmsman make a 180 degree turn and slow to Moebius one."

"Aye, sir."

The Enterprise turned smoothly and as she headed back toward the small, globe-like ships, they scattered in front of her, eventually forming a circular pattern around her.

"Impulse power now, Helmsman. How many of them are there, Scientist?"

"Fifty-three, Captain."

"Well, we'll let them look us over. So far they haven't done anything that is overtly hostile — let's return the favor."

"Captain, the Evil Witches are not going to decide that a vessel of this size can be ignored. If you fire now, you could catch most of them by surprise." The Doctor looked quite serious. "Unless, of course, you enjoy playing sitting duck."

The Captain ignored the statement. "Arm the photon torpedoes, wide range. The Helmsman, set the phases for a maximum sweep. You are not to fire except on my direct order."

For several moments, it looked as though the stalemate would be indefinitely maintained. Then simultaneous bursts of fire emerged from all the Sontaran vessels. "Photon missiles have been fired at us, Captain. Time to impact, 12 seconds," The Scientist said.

"Helmsman, Weapons Officer, fire — NOW!"

Between the wide sweep of the torpedoes and the following burst of the lasers, most of the enemy's missiles were destroyed before they reached their target. A number did get through, however, and The Captain could hear the damage reports coming in.

"Now, Weapons Officer, I want a series of photon torpedoes with a narrow burst directly at those ships. Helmsman, set the lasers on tracking and pick up any stragglers that the torpedoes miss."

The battle strategy seemed to be working effectively as thirty-five of the small vessels fell to the coordinated offense. Some of the others, however, began moving rapidly directly toward the Enterprise. They seemed to be making no effort to fire

their weapons. Their swift zig-zag motions ena-
bled them to evade any direct hits.

"They're going to smash their ships into your
shields, Captain. That will put all of their weaponry and their ships' reactors into a direct explosion
on your main defense shields," The Doctor said.

"Kamikaze?" The Captain said in amazement.

"That's what you call it — they call it fighting
for the glory of the glorious Sontaran Empire."

"Engineer, full power to the shields! Helmsman, try reaching them before they reach us.
Weapons Officer, keep the ones still on the perim-
eter under full torpedo attack."

A sudden violent rocking warned The Captain
that the kamikaze technique was proving effective.
"Damage reports, Scientist."

"That last hit was in the main power link between Engineering and secondary computer control. Exact level of damage cannot be determined..." Another blast rocked the ship, but The
Helmsman and The Weapons Officer simultaneously fired their weapons and let out a yell of ex-
altation.

"All enemy ships destroyed, Keptin."

"Very good, gentlemen. Heading 185 degrees
Helmsman. Battle stations, yellow alert status.
Damage reports, The Communications Officer."

"Sickbay reports thirty wounded — two dead."

"Life support systems damaged further in that
last attack, Captain." The Engineer was regarding
his display panels with dismay.

"How badly?"

"Less than 60% life support capability left."

"Captain," The Scientist turned from the Science console, "The computer area has also re-
ceived extensive damage to the secondary life support control memory system. With the direct

damage to life support itself, we have about two hours of life support left on the tertiary system."

Silence engulfed the bridge.

"How long will it take to repair?" The Captain asked.

The Scientist and The Engineer exchanged glances, then The Scientist spoke. "On the life support system itself, the engineering portion, about three hours, on the secondary computer memory system, about five hours."

The Captain looked over at the Doctor who was still perched on the bridge steps. "Doctor, can you get out of here in your BOX?"

"I could, but...", the Doctor gave The Captain a quizzical look.

"If we cannot complete our repairs in two hours and get the secondary system back up, this ship will begin a self-destruct sequence. So I would suggest that you be prepared to leave."

"That is one alternative, Captain, but there might be another," The Doctor said calmly. "Tell me, Engineer, Scientist, how many people would you need to complete repairs on your systems?"

The Engineer thought for a moment. "About five for the life support engineering."

"And the Computer system?" The Doctor turned to The Scientist.

"Myself and one other — the working area is small, and most of the time would be involved in testing."

"Well then, Captain," the Doctor stepped down to stand next to The Captain's chair. "If you only had a crew of, say eight — in three areas — I assume someone would have to control the bridge — and you could shut down all other areas completely — how long would your life support last?"

The Captain nearly made a remark about pointless questions, but there was something in the Doctor's tone of voice—"Engineer?"

"Ten hours."

"So that's your answer," The Doctor exclaimed gleefully, turning around.

"Doctor." The Captain tapped him on his shoulder and waited until he was facing him again. "We have a crew of 430 — and 250 additional passengers. We do not have enough space suits for everyone."

"But my BOX is on board." At The Captain's blank look he hastily continued. "Put 422 of your crew — and all of your passengers — inside her, and the rest should be able to pilot your ship and make the necessary repairs."

The Captain took a deep breath before speaking. "Doctor, are you trying to tell me that that box of yours can hold over 600 people?"

"She's quite a bit bigger on the inside than it would seem from the outside. She'll hold your people — and she has her own life support."

"Captain," The Scientist had been doing some calculations. "The time to evacuate would require full life support for the major part of the period. Estimating that against the repair time shows that we will have total oxygen depletion one hour before repairs could be completed."

"Scientist — you require less oxygen than a human." The Doctor stated.

The Scientist nodded.

"Engineer — do any of your engineers have a similar ability?"

"Aye, three of them."

"And I can manage quite comfortably with less life support than you presently provide." The Doctor turned to The Captain. "And you do have enough space suits for the humans involved?"

The Scientist turned back to the computer. The Doctor smiled at The Captain.

"Scientist?"

"The Doctor's calculations are correct, Captain. The time margin would be sufficient." He looked at the Doctor. "You would be assisting me?"

"I am somewhat familiar with computer systems."

The Captain turned to The Communications Officer. There seemed to be no doubt that the command decision had been made and he was simply to enforce it. "Order all crew and passengers except The 'Engineer's Engineers' to follow evacuation order 5 — using teleporter Room 2." He turned back to the Doctor. "Doctor, if you will open your box, we will proceed."

When they arrived, they found The Physician waiting.

"You will be taking your injured in first?" The Doctor asked.

"Yes," The Physician looked skeptically at the box. "If you're sure there's room."

"Oh yes, quite enough." The Doctor opened the door and led The Captain and The Physician into what seemed to be a very modern control room. The Captain looked around with amazement. The room was well over twice the size of the box they had entered and several doors indicated even more rooms beyond.

"Now, Physician, if you go through that door and turn right and then right again, there is an area which you will find suitable for caring for your people while we fix your ship."

He turned back to The Captain and The Scientist who were looking at the large six-sided control panel in the center of the room.

"Fascinating," said The Scientist, circling the device. "I should like to discuss its principles and functions with you sometime, Doctor."

"Well, it usually does what I want her to." The Captain had a feeling that The Scientist was not going to be able to satisfy his curiosity about this device very easily. "Why don't you start on the computer repairs, and I'll join you shortly."

"A logical suggestion." The Scientist turned and left.

"Curious little devil, isn't he?" commented the Doctor to The Captain. He apparently accepted The Captain's silence as agreement as he went on. "Now, Captain, I assume that there will be some time to evacuate those of us left after you begin your self-destruct sequence?"

"There should be."

"In case there isn't — who of your crew members could quickly learn some of these"—he motioned toward the button and lever studded panels. "To move the passengers to safety?"

The Captain smiled. The Doctor knew that he would be the one remaining on the bridge until the last minute. "Helmsman."

"Your helmsman — very good. If you would get him down here."

The Captain opened his communicator. "Helmsman, come down to the teleporter room."

"Yes, sir."

The Physician appeared at the door looking stunned. "Amazing — there's a whole city in here."

"Not quite, Fizz, but it will serve your needs. I would suggest that you begin your evacuation." The Doctor stepped over to the control panels and began setting some of the controls. The Captain and The Physician exchanged glances. It was clear from the Doctor's manner that he was accustomed to people being amazed at his BOX — and was delighted in that same amazement.

The evacuation began in an orderly fashion. After the injured had been moved in, the rest of the crew started to come. The Xenobiologist was the first inside and the Doctor turned away from the controls.

"Oh, Dorcy — if you would lead the rest of this group down the stairs, turn left, then right, and left and right, there is an area that you all should find satisfactory. Please help yourselves to the food supplies, you may have a long wait."

Lt. Stephens looked at The Captain who nodded. "Very well, Doctor."

When The Helmsman came in the Doctor was standing back from the controls apparently satisfied with what he had done.

"Helmsman." The Doctor motioned The Helmsman over to stand next to him. "I have preset the controls so that you can use these." He motioned to an array of buttons and a single lever in one of the control panel sections. "If you should have to leave quickly from here, just push these controls, and then this lever. Understood?"

"Yes, sir."

"I have programmed The BOX to land on a small Earth-type planet. You should be able to handle yourselves there."

"Helmsman," The Captain said.

"Yes, sir."

"If we do not make it back you are to follow the Doctor's orders explicitly. Keep your communicator handy and I will inform you if you are to — leave."

"Yes, sir. Good luck, Captain."

"Thank you, Lieutenant."

The Captain watched as the crew continued to file past and down the stairs. He could hear laughter coming from the lower level.

"Well, Doctor, I suggest that we get to work."

"My sentiments, exactly."

On the Bridge, seated in the helmsman's position, wearing the new X-E life support suit, The Captain had the feeling that he was piloting a ghost ship. Behind him he could hear The Communications Officer moving around as she systematically shut down life support as areas of the ship were vacated.

"All areas evacuated, sir. Life Support shut down except in engineering, computer memory control and on the Bridge."

"Have you picked up any transmissions?"

"No sir."

"Very well. Go down to the Tardis, Lieutenant. After you leave I'll shut off life support here."

With The Communications Officer gone, the 'ghost ship's feeling became even more oppressive. In an effort to dispel it, he called The Engineer to check on how the repairs were going. The Engineer informed him that his crew was progressing "as well as might be expectd" and from the tone of his voice, The Captain knew that any further interruptions would not be welcomed.

He had heard nothing from The Scientist and the Doctor. Neither one would be inclined to report until something decisive had happened and, even more so than The Engineer, would resent 'unnecessary interruptions'. The Captain decided that he could just open the communication link to the Computer Memory area. If he couldn't be there, at least he could hear what was going on.

"Are you ready to retest this bank again?" The Scientist's voice, as calm as if this were a routine maintenance check.

"Quite ready."

"Running the diagnostic program now. It should complete a successful pass in five minutes."

"Or fail in less."

"Exactly." The Scientist paused for a moment. "Doctor, why did you leave your people and go to Earth?"

"What makes you think I did that?"

"While you were unconscious in the teleporter room, I inadvertently entered into mental contact with you. That information was there."

"You're a touch-telepath?"

"Yes. I must apologize...".

"Oh nonsense, don't bother. I've had my mind invaded by far more nasty beings. Why did I choose Earth? Well, I like Earth people — compared to most of the other races I've met."

"They are a most emotional race."

"Do you think so? They're certainly not as emotional or as illogical as some I've met. They're a bloody nuisance at times and quite indomitable. They can also cause more trouble than almost any other race if you let them get started. Of course, things may be different in your universe, but what I like about the people from Earth is that by and large, they care."

"Is caring such an important thing to you?"

"Yes, when it means that the people can reach outside themselves to care for others — and especially for others not of their own species. That's extremely rare. And, somewhat surprisingly. Earth people can quite astonish you and do just that."

"And what of your own people?"

"They stopped caring about anything a long time ago — so I left."

"Did your people agree with your leaving?"

The Captain suddenly had the feeling that he was listening to a bi-level conversation. Was The Scientist trying to interrogate the Doctor — or the Doctor, The Scientist?

"Oh no, I — borrowed — The BOX and then they caught me and exiled me on Earth. Until they needed me."

"Needed you?"

"Well, they were determined not to interfere — but when you know what is going to happen, interference is sometimes needed. So I helped them out."

"And now?"

"Well, I could go back to Gallifrey, settle down, take my place on the Council, even teach in the Academy — but I'm not ready for that. There still seems to be so much more to learn. Whatever a professor might say, you don't learn — especially about yourself — in the Ivory Tower." The Doctor paused. "What about you?"

"Me?" The Captain could almost see the uplifted eyebrow.

"Yes, you. You know, one of the reasons I left was because of Oz. When the Time Lords did not interfere, I felt that a very valuable people had been lost — needlessly. I am very glad to see that my supposition was correct. Although I should not base my decision on you alone. You're half human."

"I am a Wizard."

"You mean that you've chosen the Wizard way over the Human way when you had to. I know that much about you at least — apparently the mental contact worked two ways. Why weren't

you allowed to become the best of both worlds —
instead of having to choose one over the other?"

"It is not possible to be both Wizard and Human."

"Has anyone ever tried before? I suspect that
you may be — is that board supposed to be smok-
ing?"

The Scientist muttered something that The Captain couldn't catch. "Powering down. There must
be more trouble here than our first analysis
showed."

"If the person who did your last maintenance
servicing had used the right servo-fuse, that power
surge wouldn't have effected this area at all."

"It is unfortunately a common human characteristic to use the most expedient way and avoid the
difficulty of the required way."

"Surely a characteristic not limited to humans."

A pause. "Agreed."

"That board looks pretty bad. Do you have another replacement?"

"We have no more spare memory storage mod-
ules of this type."

"Spare parts, then?"

"There is a bench testing system over there and
spare parts are available. The new memory bubble
domes will also have to be reprogrammed."

"I'll start on that now."

The Captain turned off the intercom link and
analyzed the conversation carefully. While not an
expert in the hardware maintenance of the Enterprise's computer system, he did have enough basic
knowledge to realize what had happened. During
their last scheduled maintenance, someone had
used the wrong servo-fuse in the secondary life
support memory control. The 'new' fuse was unable to prevent a power surge from coming through

and damaging what had at first appeared to be the three boards that The Scientist had identified. The Enterprise carried a number of spare boards for the computer system, but not an infinite supply.

Apparently additional damage done by the power surge had resulted in what would be a longer repair time than The Scientist had originally estimated. He looked at the chronometer. Half an hour left before the tertiary system would begin the self-destruct sequence.

The intercom sounded.

"The Captain here."

"Repairs completed in engineering. Captain. Waiting for computer control."

"Very good, Engineer. Computer Control is not yet repaired. Can you handle things down there when it is?"

"Aye, Captain."

"Then send the rest of your people to the Tardis. They'll have to wear X-E suits until they get there. The Captain to The Scientist."

"Scientist here, Captain."

"The Engineer reports engineering repairs completed. What is your estimated time for repair of the computer system?"

"Previously undetermined damage to the backplane area has necessitated rebuilding one of the spare memory boards that was damaged. I am about to replace the backplane now. Repairs should be completed in fifteen minutes."

Fourteen minutes later The Scientist's voice came over the intercom. "Diagnostic test on computer systems successfully completed, Captain. Bringing up memory systems of engineering."

"Engineer, The Scientist is bringing up your computer memory system."

"Well, if he is, Captain, there's nae anything on the asynchronous signal interface monitor."

"Scientist, did you hear that?"

"Affirmative, Captain. There appears to be an additional problem. We are investigating."

The Captain could hear the sound of someone whistling in the background as The Scientist was speaking. He wondered what the hell the Doctor could find to whistle about.

"Scientist," the Doctor said, "Look at this."

"The drivers on the fiber optic bus cable?"

"Looks like they were hit in the power surge too. What's your replacement procedure for them?"

"Difficult. We have to run a new bus cable over to engineering through the inside conduits of the ship."

"You don't use a cable connector?"

"Not with this cable. The bus bars get hung too easily."

"But you do have a spare bus cable?"

"Yes."

"Then let's get going."

"Scientist," The Captain broke in, in 12 minutes the tertiary system will default to the main computer and initiate the self-destruct."

"And we cannot bypass the main system to halt the self-destruct after that point, Captain. The Doctor will attempt to connect the cable from here to engineering. I will remain here to bring up the computer system if the connection is completed in time."

"Very well, Scientist. Doctor, you realize the risk you are taking?"

"He has already left, Captain. I can assure you that he is well aware of the risk involved."

The minutes crawled by. Five minutes left. The
Captain had a sudden vision of living out his life
on one Earth-type planet with no way to return
home and the Enterprise destroyed. It would be as
though all he had struggled for during the last five
years had counted for nothing.

Four minutes.

"Captain, the Doctor's coming through now.
I've got the cable."

Two minutes.

"Cable attached, Scientist."

"Bringing up your computer control, Engineer."
One minute.

"Secondary support system is activated, Captain. Tertiary is cut off."

The Captain looked at the chronometer. There
had been thirty seconds left. He opened his communicator. "Helmsman, as soon as all life support
is back to normal, you will evacuate the Tardis."

"Yes sir!"

In the background he could hear what seemed
to be party noises — laughing, singing. Well,
whatever the crew was doing at least they had not
had to wait alone through the agony of the last
hours. And one of The Scientist's and The Engineer's first projects when they were out of this
mess was going to be to find some way to bypass
that tertiary system self-destruct. He'd be the one
to decide what heroics were suitable to his ship.

chapter three

As the Enterprise wandered among alien stars, most of the crew were involved in repairing the damage from the storm and the subsequent battle. But all their duties were routine compared to the assignment of the Science and Engineering officers — find the way for the Enterprise to return home.

Both The Scientist and the Doctor were on this team. Its first efforts were devoted to analyzing the physics of the Enterprise's entering the alternate universe. After this had been discovered, the team could decide what needed to be done to reverse the effect.

Neither The Scientist nor the Doctor needed as much sleep as the humans on the team. The Scientist, of course, spent his time in additional work and research, but the Doctor did not seem to be so inclined.

The Captain had offered the Doctor his choice of a room on the Enterprise or staying in his box. The Doctor had chosen the Enterprise. He had pointed out that he would be in closer touch with events by being closer to the Enterprise communication system — and anyway — he'd never been on a ship like the Enterprise before.

The Captain was beginning to wonder if he was really taking the work he was supposed to be doing seriously — if he took anything seriously. He seemed to 'work' with the scientific team for only ten to fifteen minutes at a time. When The Captain sat in on the sessions he noticed that most of the Doctor's time was spent in looking at the results that the Enterprise team had generated, staring into space for a few minutes, making some minor changes in one of the currently generated equations and then leaving the room. While the team did not seem to be upset with this 'working style',

The Captain was beginning to seriously wonder just what the Doctor was contributing.

The Captain would be walking down one of the Enterprise corridors and spot the Doctor doing tricks with a yo-yo in one of the branching halls — usually with a crew member watching. He had also managed to find out from someone how to program the food computers to produce what seemed to be his major source of sustenance — the ubiquitous jellybabies. Unfortunately his programming had resulted in everyone else who ordered something getting at least one jellybaby too. The Captain suspected that the programming was no accident. He stared at the small red shape next to his fruit salad, looked at the other crew members who seemed to be happily eating theirs and decided that he had better discuss the situation with The Physician.

"Captain, I've still got 23 seriously injured people to take care of — and I can't say that anything in the Doctor's behavior has bothered me in my job."

"I just have this feeling that he may be helping himself more than us."

"Have you talked to The Scientist about it?"

"The Scientist is busy."

"Look, if there was a problem with the Doctor and the help he's supposed to be giving the team, then The Scientist would have said something. You may think that he isn't doing anything, but The Scientist may find that what he is doing is exactly what the team needs. And I can tell you this, from the tests that we've been able to run on him and from The Xenobiologist's reports, his mind is at least the equal of The Scientist's, if not better. Have you read any of the Lieutenant's reports?"

"No. Not yet."

"Well, instead of worrying about what he is or isn't doing, why don't you read them? You're expecting him to act as though he was human, and believe me, he is not."

"Excuse me. Captain."

It was The Communications Officer.

"Yes, Lieutenant?"

"Sir, the crew was wondering if we could have a party for the Doctor?"

"A party?"

"Yes, sir. We would like to thank him — all of us — for helping us with the life support problem — and lending us his box and...".

"Communications Officer, the Doctor is supposed to be trying to find out how we can get this ship back to our own universe. I hardly think that a party would be in any way appropriate."

"Come on, Captain" The Physician said. "Considering what the crew has gone through and the Lieutenant's expressions of their feelings, why don't you let her check with The Scientist and the Doctor. If they have time, it might be a good idea."

The Communications Officer was looking at The Captain expectantly. He shot an annoyed glance at The Physician. "Very well, Lieutenant. If The Scientist says that he can spare the Doctor and if the Doctor accepts, you may have your party."

"Thank you, sir."

The party started off in an orderly fashion. The Doctor turned up for the occasion in a black velvet coat, solid white scarf and top hat. The Captain assumed that this was his concession to formality.

While appropriate beverages and food were in ample supply, everyone, including the Doctor, seemed to be on their best behavior. The Captain was somewhat surprised to see The Scientist join the party, but was also relieved. The presence of his first officer usually kept an Enterprise party from turning into a raucous affair.

The Scientist had brought his Wizard's harp with him. The Captain was not surprised to see that he and The Communications Officer were going to perform. What surprised him was the performance. The Communications Officer had found an old Earth song — never popular-called "My Friend The Doctor". With somewhat revised wording, it had the Doctor laughing in one minute and the rest of the crew with him in two. From that point on, the beverage consumption increased considerably.

The Captain left half-way through the evening. The Doctor had borrowed The Scientist's lyre, with The Scientist's approval, The Captain noticed. Urged on by The Lieutenant the Doctor proceeded to teach the crew some early English drinking songs. The Captain heard that the evening wound up with a spontaneous limerick contest.

The Captain made a point of turning up in the briefing room that the Scientific team was using early the next morning. To his surprise, the whole team was there and working. A few moments later, the Doctor walked in. He seemed to be unusually somber.

"I am afraid that you people are going to have to get out of this universe."

The Scientist turned and looked at the Doctor with raised eyebrow. "Indeed?"

"Look here, Doctor, this team has been working on that problem for nearly a week now," The Captain said angrily. "What makes you say that...".

"I believe that the operative words in the Doctor's statement are 'have to'," The Scientist interrupted. The Captain looked at him and then at the Doctor in surprise. "What have you discovered?" The Scientist continued.

"I ran some studies last night in my BOX, and unless you're out of here in three weeks, there are going to be serious disturbances on the Space-Time continuum which will have the gravest consequences for several of the races native to this universe and will result in your ultimate destruction."

The Captain looked at The Scientist, who accepted the Doctor's statement. Well, at least it might get the Doctor working on the problem with more dedication than he had previously exhibited.

The Scientist turned to the computer and displayed an equation. "I believe that this is the effect that has brought us here."

The Doctor studied it. "Yes, that would do it."

"So the question is, then, how to reverse it." said The Engineer.

The team studied the figures. The Captain noticed that the Doctor seemed to be falling asleep. Then he suddenly sat up. "Of course!" He changed some of the figures in the equation.

"That would seem to be the desired effect." The Scientist said.

"And we've got just enough ruby slippers to do it." said The Engineer.

The Captain breathed a sigh of relief. At last there seemed to be a way out of the trap. And if he had to thank the Doctor for it, he would.

"Wait a minute," the Doctor said, staring intently at the display. "There's something wrong."

"I can see no error," said The Scientist.

"You're not a Time Lord," said the Doctor, still frowning at the display. "No, you can't use that, but I can't..." He got up abruptly and paced around the table. "The Matrix!"

"The Matrix?" The Scientist asked.

"Yes, the Time Lord Matrix — the summary of all Time Lord experiences — the answer's there."

"Can you obtain it?" The Scientist inquired.

The Doctor stood still for a moment, his head flung back. Then sweat broke out on his face and he stumbled back into a chair.

"Doctor," The Scientist said, "are you all right?"

"Yes — and no." The Doctor looked around the table and managed a faint smile. "I have been exposed to the Matrix, but it was contaminated, and I — I do not have full access to all the knowledge that is there."

The Scientist raised one eyebrow.

"Can you explain that more completely, Doctor?" The Captain asked.

The Doctor hesitated, then, shrugging his shoulders and exchanging a brief glance with The Scientist, began speaking. "When I became a — renegade — that portion of my mind was made inaccessible to me by the Time Lord Council. Since then...there are times when I seem to be able to access part of it, but not consistently- -and not now."

"Scientist?" The Captain knew that mind blocks of this kind were more likely to be familiar to the Wizard than to anyone else on the ship. The Scientist's eyes met The Captain's and then he turned to the Doctor, who was now staring at the computer display in obvious frustration.

"Doctor," the Doctor turned to look at The Scientist. "You state that there is a block on certain portions of your memory?"

The Doctor nodded. "It was their right to place it on me — their means of punishment."

"Does the need for the block still remain?"

The Doctor looked surprised and suddenly thoughtful. "No — no, there is no more reason for it. No one thought about it, until now."

"Can the block be removed, then?"

"Are you a Time Lord, Scientist? Is there another Time Lord on this vessel?" The Doctor got up and paced to the other side of the room. He turned back and stared at The Scientist. "Can you reach into my mind and remove it? Oh, I know that you are a touch- telepath, but can you destroy what Time Lords of the First Rank — with infinitely more experience — made?" He sat down again and this time his smile carried no humor.

"Doctor," said The Scientist, templing his hands, "you are a Time Lord. Do you believe that the block should be removed?"

There was a pause. The Doctor looked at The Scientist, obviously puzzled.

"Or do you still accept it as part of your punishment? Would your fellow Time Lords — now — consider it necessary?"

"Necessary? No, I don't think they even remember it. And until now, I really haven't needed it." He looked at the computer display again with annoyance.

"As you have observed, Doctor, I am only a touch-telepath. However, Wizards have some ability in these matters — if you can cooperate fully with me."

"You think you can remove it?"

"Not by myself, but with your support. Without your full cooperation, your own psychic abilities could interfere and — negate — our purpose."

"Then it also carries some danger for you." The Doctor looked directly at The Scientist.

"There is that possibility. The melding of one mind to another — especially between different species of varying psychic abilities — to remove or change something in one of the minds — can be hazardous. Either, or both of our minds could be lost. There is therefore a risk for you, too."

"Not a casual encounter, then." The Doctor said, and The Captain though that he almost seemed to be laughing.

"No," said The Scientist, maintaining the tension. "Is it your wish to make the attempt?"

The Doctor thought for a moment, then turned to The Captain. "Captain, is what The Scientist is proposing as dangerous to him as I think?"

"It could well be. The Scientist has never used the mind-meld casually." The Captain felt frustrated. The Doctor was acting as though he could understand everything about his first officer, and in this area The Captain knew that his knowledge was incomplete.

"If it were possible for you to remain in this universe without harm — or if the time we had to work in were longer, I might suggest a delay. As it is...what must be done?"

"I would suggest that we go to The Physician and utilize the isolation area of Sickbay."

The Physician was not pleased at the idea of the attempt, but set up the isolation area as The Scientist requested, a single bed and a chair alongside it and full medical monitoring. He looked at the room grimly.

"Captain, you realize that we could lose both of them."

"They've already discussed that possibility. Our major concern at the moment has to be to find a way to return the Enterprise to our own universe. Even the Doctor admits that."

"Even the Doctor? Captain, I think that...".

The Xenobiologist walked into the room and The Physician did not finish his statement. The Captain decided not to ask him to — if it was important, The Physician would find some time to talk to him about it. The Lieutenant eyed the isolation area with as much distaste as did The Physician. The Captain studied her for a moment. Of all the crew members, she had spent the most time with the Doctor since he had arrived. He was curious about her reaction.

"Lieutenant, you seem to share The Physician's misgivings about this experiment."

She looked up at him in amazement. "Captain, you do realize that of the two we are much more likely to lose The Scientist if the experiment fails?"

The Captain studied her. While all her records indicated a level-headed practical approach on her field missions, her reports on the Doctor had a slight tinge of gullibility. Obviously the alien Doctor had had as much effect on her as on the other crew members. "What makes you say that?"

"Because I have been studying, talking to and observing him ever since you made that my assignment. Oh, he doesn't brag about it, Captain, but obtaining such information is my field. Believe me, his experiences are not conducive to permitting an alien probe into the depths of his mind. I doubt that he would even easily tolerate such a probe from his own species."

"With The Scientist then, what could happen?"

"It all depends on the Doctor. If he truly trusts The Scientist — not just consciously, but subconsciously — enough to allow the probe to reach its intended goals then they will succeed. If he does not — or cannot — the defense mechanism of his mind would snap shut and destroy The Scientist's mind."

The Scientist entered the room as the Lieutenant had. "Is the Doctor here?"

"Not yet," The Physician answered. "The room is ready. Scientist are you certain that this is necessary? The Xenobiologist believes that it is quite dangerous."

The Scientist hesitated for a moment. "Physician, it is quite necessary." He had withdrawn into his most Vulcan image. The Captain looked at him. Could it be that the danger the Lieutenant had suggested was indeed real? He started to say something to The Scientist, when the Vulcan turned and went into the room. He sat down in the chair, hands templed, withdrawn.

"You can't stop it now, Captain." The Physician said. "It's between them."

The Doctor came in. He had discarded his coat, scarf and hat and was once again wearing a cossack-like white shirt, tweed trousers and boots.

"Is everything ready?" he said cheerfully.

The Physician nodded grimly toward the room and the silent Scientist within. "If you two are determined to proceed."

The Doctor smiled at The Physician and started to enter the room when The Xenobiologist stopped him. "Doctor." He looked down at her in surprise. "Remember you must give up the control to The Scientist." Their eyes met briefly and he nodded and went into the room.

The Captain felt a sudden chill of fear realizing that more than the life of his first officer, of his friend, lay in the hands of this alien whom he did not trust.

The Physician closed the door and turned on the intercom system. The medical monitors were on. He looked at The Captain again, shaking his head this time—"You can't stop it now, Captain."

The Doctor stopped just inside the door and looked at The Scientist. Without disturbing him he lay down on the bed, closed his eyes for a moment and then said, "Mr. Scientist, if you're ready?"

The Scientist's eyes opened slowly and he looked at the Doctor. The Doctor smiled and closed his eyes. The Scientist untempled his hands and then spread them on the Doctor's face.

"Hello, anybody home..." came the familiar words.

The Doctor's body stiffened momentarily. The Scientist's grip tightened.

"The Doctor has to drop his own telepathic blocks," The Xenobiologist whispered.

Sweat broke out on the Doctor's face and The Scientist's eyes closed tightly. The Doctor's body relaxed.

"Hello, anybody home..." The Scientist's body seemed to encircle the Doctor's although he did not move. There was silence from the room. The Captain was waiting for the outpouring of words he was used to hearing during one of The Scientist's mind merging. But nothing seemed to happen. He looked down at The Xenobiologist.

"What's going on?"

"They are both natural telepaths, Captain. This is quite unlike what you have seen before."

Perspiration gleamed on The Scientist's brow. The Doctor's body alternately tensed and relaxed.

Suddenly the eyes of the two opened and met. The Captain could almost see some kind of exchange take place.

"They are in close contact now," said The Xenobiologist. "There is only the barrier to be broken."

The eyes of the two closed again. From his own experience, The Captain remembered the feeling of another mind in his and he was not telepathic. What would it be like if that mind was attacking yours? And if you had a real ability to defend yourself — for the first time he realized that the danger The Scientist was willingly encountering was formidable. Everything depended on the ability of another to relinquish control, the whole dependent on the tightest of disciplines of the minds involved.

Discipline — and the Doctor?

"Heart rates increasing, Captain," said The Physician.

The Doctor's head began to move restlessly in The Scientist's grip. A scream emerged from the Doctor's mouth but it was The Scientist's voice that sounded.

"No, it must remain, it is the penalty./The penalty no longer exists: the penalty has been paid." The Scientist's voice now began the familiar mono-duologue. "The punishment must be complete./The punishment is no longer required. You have earned the right to be free./I am the President. The Matrix is mine. The Matrix is invaded. The Master. Death to all Time Lords. My people. There is danger. I cannot release the Matrix. I must drive out the enemy!"

"Heart rates still increasing. I don't know how much longer they can take it."

The Doctor's eyes opened and stared blindly at the ceiling. The Scientist's voice continued, a monologue this time. "Layer by layer, opening...".

Another 'voice' — this time exploding in The Captain's mind.

"Broadcast telepathy," said The Xenobiologist, wincing. "The Scientist has opened some new abilities that the Doctor has."

"The enemy has gone, the way is open."

The Scientist's hands broke contact. Grabbing the Doctor's shoulders, he caught the Doctor's eyes with his own. "You must proceed. I will not probe your knowledge."

"I must have your support, or the barrier will not be fully broken."

The Scientist paused and then resumed contact. The Doctor's eyes closed again.

"So...in this way, slowly..." the Doctor's head jerked fitfully in The Scientist's grasp. "Yes you are there, the path is open. I enter."

A stillness descended on the room.

"Heart rates going down."

The Doctor was sweating again; The Scientist seemed to be in a passive trance and The Captain was reminded of the first, involuntary contact The Scientist had made with the Doctor.

"Readings back to normal, Captain."

"If they can break the bond now..." said The Xenobiologist.

Both sets of alien eyes opened and met again. The Scientist's head jerked back. The texture of the mental voice changed. "Yes, so you have joined with us."

"No." The Scientist's hand moved to break the meld but the Doctor's hands quickly held them in place. "I am my own. I am Vulcan."

"You are still that. But you are more. It has been earned."

The Scientist's eyes closed. The Doctor's hands reached up to The Scientist's face assuming the Vulcan contact points. "Accept."

The Scientist seemed to nod in the Doctor's grasp. The Scientist's hands fell away from the Doctor, then the Doctor's from him. The Doctor came to a half sitting position. The Scientist's head was still bent, his eyes closed.

"Scientist!" cried The Captain, heading for the door. The Physician and The Xenobiologist stopped him.

"Captain," The Physician said. "You've got to let the Doctor finish now."

The Doctor took hold of The Scientist's hands which were lying limply on the bed. "Scientist," the Doctor called, then louder, and The Captain could almost feel a mental calling with the verbal, "Scientist." The Scientist's eyes opened. There was a depth to them that The Captain had rarely seen before.

"What have you given me?"

"Something more than you had before, but nothing you have not earned, were not entitled to, or more than you can handle. Why not ask what you have given me?"

The Scientist's eyes met the Doctor's. The Doctor smiled. "Scientist, I am whole again. I think that you can realize what that means. I know you — now — and I know what you risked. I risked no more than I have risked before and for no more reason. Accept my gift, my friend, and look on it as repayment for what my people failed to do in this universe for your people." The Scientist looked intently at the Doctor and nodded.

The Doctor turned to the window. "Captain, I believe that I have the solution to the problem."

The Physician opened the door.

The Scientist got up slowly. The Captain went to him. "Scientist, are you all right?"

"I believe so, Captain. It was a most unusual experience."

"Scientist," called the Doctor, "come on, we've got to get this thing solved."

"Coming."

The two left the room. The Captain and The Xenobiologist followed. The Physician decided that he was going to review the medical records of the event again.

"Lieutenant," said The Captain, walking behind The Scientist and the Doctor as they headed toward the briefing room, "What has The Scientist got now that he didn't have before?"

"It's difficult to say, Captain. Certainly some expanded knowledge or awareness that is normally unique to Time Lords. Perhaps an increase in his own telepathic abilities, perhaps some of the Doctor's sense of humor."

"Lieutenant, I do not find that particularly amusing."

"No sir, but don't you think it would be interesting?"

"No."

"Well, sir, you should be aware that it is not uncommon after such a melding as we have seen for the participants to have taken on each other's characteristics — for a time."

The Lieutenant nodded her head at the two ahead of them. The Captain saw that The Scientist was accepting one of the Doctor's jellybabies.

"Well, Lieutenant, if it gets us out of this universe and back into our own, I can tolerate anything."

"I do hope that your tolerance is up to what might happen, Captain."

Back in the briefing room, both the Doctor and The Scientist resurveyed the computer display. After a few minutes, The Doctor started smiling. Leaning on the table, he turned and looked at The Scientist.

"Do you see it?"

Still looking puzzled, The Scientist indicated an area of the equation. "There?"

"Exactly."

It seemed to The Captain that The Scientist was smiling back at The Doctor, but no change was visible except the disappearance of puzzlement. He glanced at The Xenobiologist and she nodded. So he in't the only one to have noticed something!

The Doctor started entering some new figures into the computer and the display changed. "You could probably work it out, but you can see where using that formula would have been disastrous to you."

"Indeed." The Scientist nodded.

"What was the matter?" The Captain asked.

The Doctor looked at The Scientist and gestured as if giving him the center stage.

"The time factor, Captain."

"Time factor?"

"Yes, in transferring between universes there is always an inherent time factor. Had we tried to return to our universe using the original formula, we would have arrived in the correct universe, but 300 years before the time we disappeared." The Scientist turned to the Doctor, one eyebrow cocked.

"A somewhat simplified explanation, but correct. With this change, you should return within five minutes of the time you left and you will not need to return to the Sontaran area."

The Engineer had been eyeing the changed equation and suddenly spoke, "Captain, I canna say that this willna do the trick, but we dinna hae the power for it."

The Scientist and the Doctor surveyed the equation. The Scientist nodded, "The Engineer is correct, Captain. The new formula calls for at least one third again as much power as our present ruby slippers will give us."

"Could we reverse the polarity?" The Doctor asked.

"Doctor, ye canna be serious," exclaimed The Engineer.

"I do not think that will work — this time." The Captain could have sworn that The Scientist was trying to keep from laughing.

"Well, well, never a solution but another problem," said the Doctor. "What will you need to solve this one?"

The Engineer had apparently been doing some calculating too. He answered immediately, "At least six more ruby slippers. I can jury-rig a system so that they could give us the power when we need it, but we've got to have the ruby slippers."

The Captain noticed, without a great deal of surprise, that everyone in the room turned to the Doctor. Well, after all, this was his universe, and he seemed to like playing the deus ex machina and pulling the Enterprise out of difficulty.

"Well, Doctor, where can we get the ruby slippers?"

"There is a planet in this area which has a supply of ruby slippers."

"Can we buy — or trade — with them to get the slippers?"

I don't know," the Doctor sat forward pensively, templing his hands in front of his face. The Captain felt a slight shock at this Scientist-like gesture. He glanced over at The Scientist and felt his shock compound as he saw that The Scientist was leaning back in his chair looking ready to put his feet up on the table. He felt The Xenobiologist touch him gently on the arm and heard her whisper "Tolerance, Captain."

The Doctor untempled his hands and stood up.

"This planet is highly unusual, even for this universe. Apparently, a humanoid race started to settle it about a thousand years ago. It should have been a normal settlement — everyone working together in the early years, wars and other problems coming along later — you know the patterns."

The Captain saw The Xenobiologist nodding — apparently what the Doctor was saying was something familiar to CS&C.

"Instead a split occurred very early. Some of the colonists were determined to maintain a high level of technology in spite of almost impossible difficulties, and others wanted to live the basic 'back to nature' life that seemed to fit the planet."

"So we have to deal with one group or the other?" The Captain asked.

"More than that. There were certain aspects about the planet which caused an abnormal development of what you call PSI powers in some of the people — on both sides. The 'back to nature' group accepted these and encouraged them. The technologists ignored and repressed them. The two groups have now developed two totally opposite ways of dealing with any type of problem."

"I don't see that that makes a difference." The Captain felt that the Doctor was seeing problems where there weren't any.

"It wouldn't — if it hadn't been for the invasion."

"Invasion?"

"Yes — an utterly ruthless race recently tried to conquer the planet and both sides ultimately joined together to defeat the invaders."

"Then we only have one side to deal with."

"Well, when the would-be conquerors left, they wanted to take revenge on the planet and the people that had withstood them — to prove that ultimately they could win. You know the type."

The Captain saw The Scientist nod out of the corner of his eye and glancing over at him saw that his feet were up on the table now. He was about to say something when a kick on the skins diverted him. He glared at The Xenobiologist who was staring innocently at the Doctor.

"At any rate, Captain," the Doctor went on — The Captain was certain that he had missed none of the byplay, "the invaders placed several fission type bombs around the planet in such a fashion that at irregular periods for the next five years the orbits will decay and a bomb will come down."

"And if they simply explode the bomb, they'll create a ring of radiation around the planet that will eventually destroy them," The Engineer said.

"Exactly."

"Sounds like we might be able to help, " The Captain said.

"We can certainly remove the bombs from their orbits and dispose of them somewhere else safely," said The Engineer.

"Would that be a sufficient trade for ruby slippers?" The Captain asked.

"Possible," the Doctor seemed to be studying his hands again. "Does your Directive prevent you from helping other people?"

"No. Just from interfering with the natural development of an indigenous culture," responded The Xenobiologist.

"Well, on this planet, the ruby slippers are mined and controlled by the back to nature group — the Norms, as they call themselves. They can use the ruby slippers to expand and amplify their psychic abilities. And it was one of their cities that was hit by the first bomb that fell." The Doctor looked at The Captain expectantly.

"Are you suggesting that we supply medical aid?"

"Yes, can you agree to that?"

The Captain responded without hesitation, "Yes."

"Very well, then, let's get to the planet and do some horse tradings. The coordinates..." The Doctor punched up some figures on the computer display.

"What," said The Scientist sitting upright again, "is the name of this planet?"

"Lightunder," said the Doctor. He started out the door and stopped. "One more thing, you know I told you that some of the people had psychic abilities?"

"Yes," The Captain failed to see why the Doctor was reemphasizing a point.

"Well, apparently the ability is tied to a recessive gene, because you can usually recognize a psychic by their physical appearance too."

"How?" The Xenobiologist asked. The Captain supposed that such an item might be of interest to a xenobiologist.

"By the color of their hair." The Doctor started out the door.

The Lieutenant looked puzzled for a minute and then shouted, "What color is it?"

The Doctor's head reappeared around the corner. His grin reminded The Captain of the Cheshire Cat in the old story.

"Green." He said and disappeared.

The estimated time of arrival to the planet the Doctor had specified was two days.

On the first day, The Captain ordered a Class One check of the ship. While that kept the crew busy for a while, and everything checked out in excellent condition, by evening things were back in their normal hurry up and wait mode. The Captain was concerned about the crew's morale. They had, after all, been overdue for R & R before starting the return trip to Earth, and had had a succession of emergencies in a rather short time.

He spent the evening walking around the ship, visiting areas where the crew was stationed and gathered.

In the gym The Helmsman was practicing what appeared to be a new and difficult series of fencing moves. "Improving your technique, Helmsman?"

"Yes sir. The Doctor showed me some offensive moves that I'd never heard of before. The problem is to try to master them."

"The Doctor?"

"Yes sir, he said he learned them from a Captain in Cleopatra's army."

The Captain watched as The Helmsman went back to his practicing. He knew his history well enough to know that at the time of Cleopatra the swords used were not the epee The Helmsman used. But The Helmsman seemed to find the whole thing credible, so The Captain decided not to try to argue about it.

Passing through the Engineering section, The Captain saw that The Engineer seemed to be involved in analyzing a silver object about 13 centimeters long and 3 centimeters in diameter. He knew that The Engineer had been working on the designs which would implement the extra ruby slippers. He walked over to see what was going on. The silver object was something he had never seen before.

"Something new, Engineer?"

"Aye, Captain. It's a Sonic Screwdriver, and it's a beautiful wee bairn."

"A Sonic Screwdriver?" The term sounded more like an exotic bar concoction than something to engage the professional interest of his Chief Engineer.

"Aye, it's the Doctor's."

"The Doctor's?"

"I've been trying to persuade him to let me look at that box of his, but he doesna seem to want to let me do that."

"So how did you get this — Sonic Screwdriver?"

"Well, he says that if I can duplicate it, then I can look at the box."

"Can you?" The Captain was confident that nothing mechanical was beyond The Engineer's skills.

"Not yet. Oh, it's a bonnie wee bairn. So far I've found thirty uses for it, but I canna yet make another one."

"Did The Doctor make it?"

"Well, he designed it."

"Well, Engineer, if you keep at it, you'll find the secret."

"Secret! Nae, Captain, this is pure engineering genius. And an honor it is to be working on it."

The Captain walked out shaking his head. The Doctor certainly seemed to have found the way to keep The Engineer away from his box.

One of the Rec rooms had been turned into what The Lieutenant explained to The Captain as the site of the Starfleet Yo-Yo Championships.

"Where did all the yo-yos come from Lieutenant?"

"Oh, the Doctor gave them to us."

"Did he set up the rules of this — competition?"

"Set them up? No sir. He told us what the rules were — back on Earth."

"Will he be participating?"

"No sir. He said he'd already won his championship in 1923."

The Captain watched a Munchkin ensign attempt a 'walk the doggie'.

"All the Munchkins are very good at this, sir. They seem to have a knack for it."

"That would certainly be helpful."

"If you'll excuse me, sir, my turn is coming up."

"Of course."

On his way to Rec room 4 The Captain mulled over what he had seen. His crew was alert, happy and there certainly seemed to be no cause for alarm. He decided he would see if The Scientist would join him for a game of chess. Certainly they could both use the break.

In Rec room 4 The Scientist was already playing chess-with The Doctor.

The Captain walked over and looked at the board. It was obviously near the end of the game and as The Captain neared them The Doctor made a move.

"Check and mate, I believe."

The Scientist studied the board. "You have learned the game well."

"It's much more challenging than the one dimensional version I'm used to. I'll have to teach it to Canine when I get him fixed."

"Canine?" The Captain asked.

"My dog."

"Your dog?—plays chess?" The Captain looked at The Scientist in hopes of some amplification of the strange statement.

"Actually, Canine is a highly sophisticated robot," The Scientist said, resettling the pieces on the boards. The Captain relaxed. At least his first officer was back to normal.

"However," The Scientist went on, "he is really a very good dog."

chapter four

The Doctor had looked slightly disappointed at The Scientist's mundane explanation of Canine and now smiled across the board at him. He was shocked to see his first officer smile back.

"Scientist?"—The Scientist turned to look at him, his face expressionless again. "Um — would you say that the Doctor plays as illogically as humans?"

"Captain," one Vulcan eyebrow raised, "the Doctor's mind works in a unique fashion. I would not compare the processes."

"Would you care to play the next game, Captain?" asked the Doctor, starting to get up from his chair.

"No, no." The Captain motioned him back down. "Scientist and I play quite often."

Of course, as their mission was ending, he and The Scientist...Well, he though, at least the Doctor was out of mischief. He went back to his cabin determined to have a talk with The Physician the next day.

"Fizz, are you sure that The Scientist is all right?"

"Captain, he's fine. He just had me give him a complete physical."

"He asked for one?"

"Captain, it was the — logical — thing to do. He wanted to be sure that there were no after-effects from that mind-merge experiment. Made me give the Doctor one too. Not that I needed to add any more of those strange readings to my records."

"Don't you find that — strange?"

"Before the whole thing happened — yes. Now — well, I don't know what you're worried about, but The Scientist is healthier — in body and mind — than I've ever seen him. What are you so wor-

ried about?"

"Fizz, I don't know. I just have this strange feeling that something is wrong — with the ship — and that the Doctor is somehow related to it."

"Well, he certainly has done nothing but help us since we got in this mess. The crew likes him, I like him and The Scientist likes him. You're the only one having problems dealing with him, Captain...."

"Physician, Lieutenant Caffrey is fibrillating again." The Nurse called from inside one of the sickbay areas."

"Damn — Captain, I want to talk to you about this after I take care of my patient."

The Captain stared glumly at the door as The Physician left. He could not believe that he was the only one out of step. Every feeling that he'd learned to rely on told him that something was wrong.

"Captain." It was The Helmsman on the intercom from the Bridge.

"The Captain here."

"Coming into the Lightunder system."

"I'm on my way up."

Orbiting the planet the next day, the selected landing party met in one of the briefing rooms.

The Xenobiologist has been working with the Doctor gathering information about the planet through a linkup of The BOX and the Enterprise sensors. "Luckily the Techies — the technologists — and the Norms are still speaking to one another," she said. "We don't want to get involved in a civil war. Only one bomb has fallen on a populated area — the first one. It destroyed the Norm city of Metebe and left strong radioactive after effects. The population in the area is suffering from radia-

87

tion exposure. The Norms were able to deflect the second bomb as it was falling, but lost five of their best telekinetics to do it. The area it landed in was unpopulated, but we will need to do a clean-up of the radiation. The bombs are too distant for the Norms to move them further out, or keep them up, and the Techies don't have a clear enough understanding of how the internal mechanism works to enable the Norms to defuse one as it comes down. They are in a desperate situation and they know it. However, they are very proud and will resent any intrusion even though it is intended to be helpful."

"Full diplomacy, then, Lieutenant," said The Captain. He noticed that The Physician was staring at him but he had been too caught up in plans for the planetary contact — including a possible use of the Doctor's BOX as the 'hospital base' to get back to talk to him. It would have to wait.

"Diplomacy in spades, Captain, if we hope to accomplish anything."

"Doctor, if you're ready?"

The Doctor had his feet up on the table and his hat over his head. The Captain was convinced that he had been sleeping.

"What — oh yes — are we ready?"

"We will be beaming down into the meeting room of the capital city of the Techies. The leaders of both sides should be there." The Scientist said.

As the group materialized, The Captain could see the surprise of the men and women in the room. He hoped that this display of superior technology would give them a bargaining advantage. He looked around at the people. Even from their clothing he could distinguish between the two groups. The Techies wore military type one piece suits, and the Norms used leather and fur garments. All carried swords.

"We have come in peace." The Captain said, spreading his hands to show the absence of weapons. "We would offer our assistance...".

"We do not wish the assistance of aliens!" shouted one of the Norms, a short, but powerfully built man. Mutters from the others in the room indicated that they agreed. The Captain was starting to frame another sentence when the Doctor abruptly stepped forward. He calmly surveyed the group and said "I am the Doctor, a Time Lord of Gallifrey. We have determined that without our intervention your planet will be destroyed in 16 months. We have decided that we will intervene to save you — for a price."

The Captain found the arrogance in the Doctor's tone unmistakable.

The man who had refused The Captain stared at the Doctor. His green hair seemed to bristle. "A Time Lord. We have heard of you." A small polished slipper that he wore on the inside of his left wrist began to glow as he lifted his hand. When his hand was level with his eyes the slipper suddenly flashed. The Captain felt what seemed to be a momentary pressure on his mind and heard The Scientist take a sudden deep breath. The Doctor seemed amused.

"So, it is true. What is your price? And who are these people with you who are not Time Lords?"

"Our price is six large ruby slippers — the size you do not use because you cannot control them." The scorn in the Doctor's voice hung in the air. "These people have been chosen to assist me."

"What do you offer us?"

"Medical help for those of your people suffering from the effects of the first explosion. And we will remove the remaining devices from your skies."

"Will you treat our people in our own land — without bringing in large machines?"

"We will land our own dwelling place where you specify. The machines we use will be no more to you than a black box that makes noise. What machines we have in our dwelling place will be of no concern to you."

"Will you teach us so that we may avoid something like this happening again?" one of the Techies asked.

The Doctor looked at him as if he was some kind of lower species of insect. "We will teach you enough to better defend yourselves." The Doctor looked at the group. "Do you accept our offer?"

"We must discuss..." murmured the Techie.

"What is there to discuss!" said the Norm. "This is a Time Lord and he speaks the truth. Must we discuss if we wish to live or die?"

There was no dissenting voice from the group as they looked ruefully at each other. The Norm turned back to the Doctor.

"Very well, Time Lord. We will agree to your bargain. But those of you who come on our land must agree to abide by our customs."

"Agreed." said the Doctor. "Where do you wish us to place the medical treatment center?"

"We have established a place of healing in Besteco."

"Then we will land there. After we remove the devices orbiting your planet, we will send people to meet with you." The Doctor nodded at the Techies.

One of the Techies stepped forward. He was tall, with blond hair and a beard. "I am Lif d'Lewis, head of my people. We will be glad to learn all that you are willing to teach us."

The Doctor nodded an acknowledgment of the Techie's statement. The Captain could not help thinking that if they had to deal only with this man and his people instead of the feisty Norm who had taken over, the whole thing could have been handled better.

"Captain, if you will call for the beam-up." The Doctor turned back to the Norm. "Alert your people at Besteco. We will be there in one hour." He turned and nodded at The Captain, obviously concluding the conversation. The Captain opened his communicator. He felt as though he was an Ensign again.

"Captain to Enterprise, beam up landing party."

As the teleporter beam picked up the landing party, The Captain felt a sudden surge of anger. What right did the Doctor have to step in like that! He could feel the emotion pulsing through him as the group materialized in the Enterprise. As he turned to the Doctor prepared to express his anger, The Scientist stepped forward and said, "An excellent job, Doctor. I believe you accomplished everything we desired."

"Even what you offered the Techies is well within the limits of the Directive. How did you know that was the proper way to approach them?" The Xenobiologist asked. The Doctor looked slightly surprised.

"It was the — logical — thing to do." He smiled at The Scientist, shaking his head slightly.

The Captain felt as if a bucket of ice water had been dumped on him. The Scientist and the Lieutenant were right. What they had wanted done was done — so why did it matter WHO had done it? Suppressing an uneasy feeling of having been in the wrong, he turned to The Physician. "Fizz, are you and your medical team ready?"

"As ready as we can be, Captain. It's a good thing that we'd already expected that we'd have to use the Doctor's BOX as our base. We've installed some of our medical computers and laboratory equipment. The Doctor and The Scientist have also arranged to implement a direct link between the BOX's computer system and our science computer."

"You're satisfied with the arrangement, then?"

"They're better than most I've had to work with under the Directive on a primitive planet."

"Fizz," said the Doctor. "If you will have your medical team at The BOX in — say — fifteen minutes? The Xenobiologist and I want to review some of the customs of the local people. Dorcy has a feeling that certain aspects of the local culture were not emphasized strongly enough in the standard briefing tape she made earlier. The Norms are very set in certain ways and we cannot afford to offend them."

"We'll be there."

"Captain, if you are planning on coming down to the planet, you should hear this." The Doctor said.

"I'll have to get it later, Doctor. At the moment we need to get this ship ready to dispose of those orbital bombs."

The Doctor looked at The Captain and, with a slight smile, nodded. "Of course, Captain."

Beaming down the box was a learning experience for The Lieutenant under The Scientist's guidance. Apparently something of the unique nature of the box had to be calculated for during transportation and The Captain was thankful that the beam-down with his crew aboard was successful.

He looked at the now empty teleporter pads and turned to The Scientist.

"Why didn't the Doctor take the box down on its own, Scientist? Wouldn't it have been simpler?"

"With the box in its present condition, there is always the chance that it might not land where it was directed."

"You mean that the Doctor can't control it?"

"His level of control of the box suits him, Captain. In this situation, I preferred that we handle the transportation."

"Scientist, there are some things that I simply do not understand."

"Indeed, Captain?" The Captain looked over and saw that his first officer was looking at him expectantly.

"Not now, Scientist, we've got some bombs to get rid of."

"But of course, Captain."

The removal and defusing of the orbiting bombs was time consuming but relatively simple for the Enterprise crew. The defused bombs were dumped into a sun of a nearby uninhabited planetary system. The Captain was pleased to see that his crew was handling the situation in their usual efficient fashion. With the disruptive influence of the Doctor removed, things were going to return to normal. Within a week the Enterprise had returned and was orbiting Lightunder again.

The Engineer and a team of Enterprise engineers and selected members of the SC&C group beamed down to meet with Lyr d'Lewis. Another group was assigned to 'clean up' the unpopulated area of the second explosion. The Captain decided to go down with The Scientist to see how the medical group was getting along.

In the teleporter room, The Scientist placed a small black box on the teleporter console.

"Lieutenant, initiate signaling sequence 21CQ305260." The Scientist said.

"Yes sir."

"What's that all about, Scientist?" The Captain asked as they walked toward the teleporter pads.

"Without the adjustment and amplification that device provides for our signals, we would not be able to beam down inside the box. The Doctor has specifically requested that any landing party at Besteco beam down directly into the box and await further contact."

"Are you saying that without this device, we wouldn't be able to transport into the box?"

"The box has unique defensive capabilities."

The Captain sighed. He was back in the strange world of the Doctor's again. They materialized inside the box control room just as the Doctor was coming in through the outside door.

"Oh, Scientist," he said, "I'm glad you're here. Come on down to the workshop. I want you to look at something."

The Scientist and the Doctor had started through one of the other doors when the Doctor stuck his head back through the door.

"Captain — don't leave the box until you check with The Xenobiologist." Then he disappeared again.

The Captain waited for some time, his impatience growing. Other members of the medical team came hurriedly through the box control room, apparently to and from the area where the Doctor and The Scientist were. They barely acknowledged his presence. The Xenobiologist did not appear.

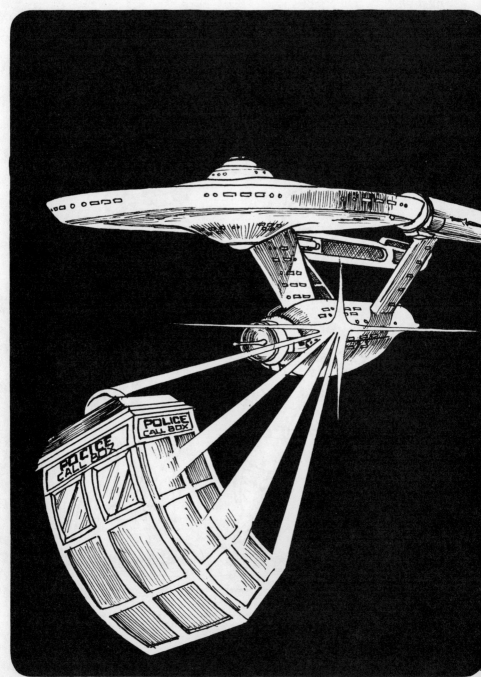

His patience finally exhausted, he decided that it would not hurt to go and look for the Lieutenant, or preferably, The Physician. They probably just wanted to re-emphasize some of the local customs. He had already seen the briefing tape twice and had been taking care of himself on alien planets several years longer than the Lieutenant. If they wanted to make some special point, he'd find them and let them make it.

As he stepped out of the box, he noticed that the 'hospital' seemed to be a converted large stone building. The box had actually been located in a room in the building.

The other rooms he saw as he walked down the hall were filled with patients. The medical personnel, both his own people and some from the native population seemed to be constantly busy. He could not see The Physician or The Xenobiologist anywhere.

At length his wanderings took him to the front door of the building. The sunlight and open air outside looked inviting after the closed-in aura of the hospital. He even seemed to be experiencing a slightly nauseous feeling from the strange pungency. All hospitals smell, he thought. He decided to step outside and look around.

Leaning on the beast-shaped stone structure at the foot of the hospital steps, he looked out at what seemed to be a town square. There were shops on three sides and the normal activity of people going in and out with and without parcels. Horses — or a very close facsimile of the Earth animal, except for the cloven hooves and horn — and carriages were tied up by the stores.

He took a deep breath of the planet's air. It tasted good.

He noticed a girl — a young woman — standing by one of the shops, apparently waiting for someone. He looked at her intensely.

Her hair was a dark green, so dark as to be almost black. The slight breeze blowing against the lightweight rose fabric of her ankle length gown outlined a figure of delightful proportions.

She suddenly looked up at him, revealing dark black eyes formerly masked by thick and curly downcast eyelashes. Her skin was fair, highlighted by a natural rose shading on her cheeks and lips which The Captain could tell owed nothing to artifice. She met his gaze for an instant and then cast her eyes down again momentarily. He was not surprised when, after a brief moment, the open and provocative gaze met his again.

How lovely she was — and would be on any planet he had ever visited. The rose of her cheeks seemed to deepen and a faint smile appeared on her lips and the black eyes seemed to sparkle. He could not speak to her, he remembered that from the briefing tape, but he continued to smile into those brilliant eyes and it seemed that his smile was echoed back to him. It had been a long time for him, and his thoughts became more specific. Her body and his, meeting, blending...A horrified look appeared in the lovely eyes and she turned and ran into the shop. Well, you can't win them all, he thought wistfully.

He felt slightly dizzy and was turning to go back into the hospital when he saw The Scientist, The Physician and the Doctor coming out.

"Captain," said The Physician, "Have you seen The Xenobiologist?"

"Not yet, Fizz." He replied, smiling.

The Scientist and The Physician exchanged glances of — irritation? Why should seeing The

Xenobiologist be such an important matter?

"Blithering idiot," said the Doctor. "You'd better get back inside and let us look at you."

The Captain bristled. What right did the Doctor have to give such an order and, anyway, they could just as well look at him out here...

There was a commotion across the street. The four on the hospital steps turned.

Three men were approaching rapidly. The Captain saw the girl he had been looking at being bundled into a carriage with some other women.

The men paused, face to face now with the Doctor and the Enterprise crew. The Captain recognized one as the Norm who had been present at the meeting in the Techie capital.

The Norm looked at the Doctor. "You said that your people would abide by our customs."

"I did."

"This man," he motioned to The Captain, "has violated one of our women."

The Doctor seemed to take a deep breath. The Scientist and The Physician simultaneously exclaimed "Captain!"

The Captain looked at them and, with a shock, realized that they seemed to be accepting the justification of the charge.

"Fizz, Scientist — I just got here!" He felt a wave of dizziness sweep over him.

"Time is relative, Captain," said the Doctor. He turned to the man who had stated the charge. "You are Raul d'Colm'n, head of the clan d'Colm'n, and you are making this charge?"

"On behalf of my kinswoman, Namona d'Colm'n, I am."

"The one charged has the right of defense by challenge."

"With swords and knives." d"Colm'n looked scornfully at the Doctor.

"Will your clan accept the challenge of defense?"

"We will — and the best of our warriors will face this pervert personally."

"Where will the challenge be?"

"In the hall of the d'Colm'n. We will take the accused there now."

"I am liegelord to the accused. I shall go with him."

"It is your right. But only you as liegelord may do so. And you must leave all of your alien machines behind. We have extra horses; we will leave now. The challenge will be on the morrow."

The Captain found himself clinging to the sculpture. The dizziness seemed to be getting worse. Was this a dream?

The three d'Colm'n went back across the square. The Captain heard the sound of a tricorder behind him. He turned and saw The Physician and The Scientist looking at something on the screen of The Physician's tricorder. They both looked grim. The Doctor was coming out of the door carrying a sword and knife in a curious double scabbard and a leather jacket. He started for The Captain when The Physician stopped him.

Odd, the three seemed to be blurring — had he been drinking? They were talking. He heard the words but didn't want to bother trying to make sense out of them. The stone sculpture felt cool and comfortable.

"How serious is the challenge?"

"Very. Don't worry about it, I'll take care of it. He'll be back to you in two days."

Now that was the Doctor talking — he'd take care of it! He thought he could handle anything.

Well, The Captain could handle this, and his ship, and his crew, and his friends. He'd show them — handle this situation the way he had all the others there had been and everything would be fine.

The blurring seemed to be getting worse and he could barely recognize The Physician's shape coming toward him with a hypospray. He felt the hypospray going in, but nothing seemed to happen. The Doctor was putting a leather jacket on him. He tried to shrug it off. He wasn't cold; it was too hot on this damn planet. The Scientist's face suddenly came into focus and he realized that the Vulcan was pulling the jacket back on him.

"Captain?"

Was that The Scientist? He hadn't called him Captain in a long time. He tried to listen.

"Captain — you must do what the Doctor says. Do you understand?"

The Captain nodded. He felt The Scientist removing his laser and communicator. Of course, even The Scientist wanted the Doctor to be in charge.

"Doctor, there is a problem."

The Doctor had been getting some medical supplies from The Physician and was stuffing them in his pockets.

"Problem, Scientist?" The Captain felt the blue eyes focus on him. He turned away from the penetrating look. "If he doesn't cooperate, we will both be lost."

The Scientist turned back to The Captain who had now decided that he wouldn't look at any of them. The dizziness seemed to be passing, but the feeling of estrangement continued. He felt the Vulcan's hands grasping his head, turning it so they were face to face, the hands shifting into the 'meeting of the minds' position.

"No Scientist!" Had he said that, or just thought it? The Vulcan's eyes, now close to his, seemed to soften, but he felt The Scientist's mind enter his.

You must return to us alive. You must do what the Doctor tells you to do.

He has turned all of you away from me. He is an enemy.

He is not an enemy. He is our friend.

He has fooled all of you. He has not fooled me.

Captain! You must not think that. Now, look back on what has happened. Review all of it. Is our friendship so fragile that you can no longer trust me?

I trust you.

Then trust the Doctor also. If you do not, we will never meet again.

Your word?

My word.

An alien touch — mind?—entered.

They are returning.

The Scientist broke off the meld. "He is in your hands, Doctor."

The Doctor nodded.

The dizziness had gone now and The Captain was able to get on the horse without help. As they rode off, the Doctor rode next to The Captain. They were both surrounded by armed men.

Raul led the group through rough paths and rocky trails. The Captain spent most of his time trying to stay on the horse. He was thankful when they arrived at their destination.

A heavily fortified, castle-like structure stood on top of one of the smaller mountains. He noticed banners flying from the turrets which matched the banners that several members of the party were carrying. The emblem displayed a white sheep on a yellow and blue striped background with a bell inside a double ring in one corner.

"Why a sheep?" He could not resist asking the Doctor as they got off their horses in the courtyard of the castle.

The Doctor glanced at him. "You don't know the sheep on Lightunder. It is quite an appropriate emblem for this clan."

The armed men escorted them to a large chamber. They left and Raul stood facing the Doctor. The Captain's knees felt oddly weak again and he sat down in one of the high-backed chairs.

The little man looked up at the Doctor and said, "While you are not of our people, we will give you the guesting appropriate to the challenge."

"You honor us," said the Doctor.

Raul looked over at The Captain. "Is your man not well?"

"It has been a long trip and he has drunk too heavily."

Raul seemed to be weighing the Doctor's words. The Captain debated protesting that he had not been drinking at all but the effort seemed too much.

"That is no excuse." Raul made the statement definitive.

"It was not given as one."

Raul nodded as though the answer satisfied him.

"Food will be sent. The challenge will be fought at cock's crow on the morrow. You will be summoned."

"Who will be fighting for the d'Colm'n?"

"I shall be."

"As is my right, I shall fight for my liegeman."

"As you wish. I would not have thought him worth it."

Raul turned and left the room. The Captain suddenly realized that he limped. Then the significance of the last remarks sank in and lethargy was swept away.

"What do you mean, you're fighting for me? I can fight for myself!"

"Captain," the Doctor came over and forced The Captain back into the chair. He leaned over one arm. "How skilled are you at fighting with sword and knife?"

"I've used those weapons."

"Against the most skilled man on a planet which only uses those weapons?"

"Him?"

"Captain — you must not judge by appearances. For all his size and injured leg, he is the best that this planet has produced. You could not win against him."

The dizziness seemed to be returning. The Captain shook his head, trying to clear it. "Can you?"

"Yes — most likely. It is our only chance. How do you feel?"

The words seemed to come out of a distance. The Scientist had said 'trust him'.

"Weak and dizzy. What's going on?"

The Doctor began rummaging in the pockets of his coat and pulled out one of The Physician's hyposprays. The Captain heard it hiss against his arm.

"That should help. I'll wake you when the food comes."

The Captain awoke to find himself supported by the Doctor's arm. He was lying in one of the beds. The Doctor was spooning some kind of broth into his mouth. He started to pull away but then relaxed.

"Well, I'm glad to see that The Scientist got through to you." The broth seemed to be finished and the Doctor offered The Captain a chunk of some type of whole grain bread and propped him up in the bed. "Eat as much of it as you can. You need the energy." The Doctor sat back in a chair and took out a bag of jellybabies.

"Doctor — what the hell is wrong with me?"

"You didn't see The Xenobiologist before you left The BOX, did you?"

"No. I...".

"You didn't really think that it was necessary. Well, because you didn't see her, you didn't receive the immunity injection you humans require for the current virus mutation that's floating around. So now you've caught the disease."

"Then the shots I've been getting are part of the cure."

"The shots aid in relieving the symptoms, but we have not yet found the cure. The mortality rate is 97%."

The Captain suddenly lost his appetite. The Doctor reached out and took the remaining bread out of his hand.

"You know, Captain, there are times when it pays to listen to someone you don't like."

"Doctor...I..."

"Don't try to excuse it, Captain. I can understand what happened. I should have recognized it earlier. You're about to wind up your mission in a blaze of glory, when you get sidetracked into this." The Doctor made a vaguely circular motion with his hand.

"I certainly wasn't prepared for anyone like you."

The Doctor chuckled. "But surely, Captain, you must realize that one of the things I did, inadvertently, was to trigger some of the fears you have about what will happen when you do complete your mission."

"Changes."

"Yes — changes." the Doctor said cheerfully, "Separation and loneliness. And you are so bound to your ship that the separation..." he became oddly pensive. "I think that you had better tell me what happened in the square that got us into this."

The Captain related the events as he recalled them, noticing that the dizziness and the fog seemed to be approaching again. As he finished his story he felt the hypospray against his arm.

The hissing sound of another hypospray awoke him in the morning.

"The Physician will not be thrilled with what I'm doing, but you've got to stay on your feet during the next several hours. Here, drink this." The Doctor held out a small vial of liquid. Without hesitating, The Captain drank it. The effect was immediate; a feeling of normalcy returned. He got out of the bed and saw that the Doctor was strapping on the double scabbard. He was wearing only the spotless flowing white shirt, tweed pants and boots. The rest of his clothes were laid in a neat pile. "Can you carry those?"

"Yes."

The Doctor pulled the sword from the scabbard and looked at it. It was a curious shape. One edge curved slightly while the other was straight. Both edges were honed to a fine sharpness. The strange blend of direct and curved line met in an elongated point.

"That's an unusual sword," The Captain commented.

"It's designed for great efficiency. Because of the curved edge, you gain an impetus to your blow if you decide to swing at your enemy — but the point still allows for the thrust." His voice seemed quite academic. "Do you see these grooves?" He indicated two channels in each side of the weapon. "If you should sink your weapon into your enemy to that depth and then quickly remove it, a suction is created — which causes an even greater loss of blood than in the flat sided weapon."

With a sudden intuition, The Captain said, "You don't like weapons, do you?"

"Aren't all men supposed to enjoy the fight?"

"You don't even travel armed — you were completely defenseless when you came out of the box."

"It has been my experience that if you go about armed, more people are apt to attack you than otherwise. You humans seem to feel an absolute compulsion to have some weapon or another on you."

"I think that for us it is a form of security — that we expect more attacks than welcomes. To leave all weapons behind — consistently — would be a step beyond our understanding of ourselves."

"I didn't think that you were a philosopher."

"Not a philosopher, but as a Starship Captain I have to have some understanding of my crew — and most of them are human, like me." The Captain smiled wryly.

The Doctor looked at The Captain with puzzlement and The Captain wondered what he had said that had surprised the Doctor in some fashion.

A knock sounded at the door.

"Our escorts." said the Doctor.

chapter five

They were led down into a large circular hall. The seating around the sides slope so that all could have a good view. The entrances from the front and back reminded The Captain unpleasantly of the ancient Roman gladiatorial contests.

The Doctor and The Captain stepped unto the floor, their escorts falling back. The Doctor motioned to The Captain. "Stand back away from the combat area and do not interfere — whatever happens. If I am killed, they will be required to let you go."

"Then you are not certain about winning."

"Of course I am," said the Doctor huffily. "The probability that I can defeat Raul is at least — 90%." He seemed to think for a minute and then said with what seemed to The Captain to be incorrigible honesty, "Well, 70% anyway." He started out for the center of the room and then turned back to The Captain, smiling. "At least it's 100% better than yours!"

As The Captain watched the Doctor turn and walk into the center, he realized that he was nearly laughing. All his fears and distrust of the Doctor seemed to have vanished. The Doctor was what he was — and that was worthy of all the trust that The Scientist and The Physician had placed in him, that now The Captain would place in him. If he had been the better swordsman, the Doctor would have made him fight his own battle. As it was, the Doctor would fight for him.

Raul emerged from the other door. He was dressed in full swordsman's outfit — leather, silver, the sword and the knife. The two men accompanying him stepped to one side and Raul, his green hair blazing, walked to the center.

A gong sounded and both men drew their weapons. The fight began slowly, both men cir-

cling, taking cautious feints at each other, looking for weaknesses.

When the action finally began, The Captain had a few uneasy moments as the Doctor seemed to be outclassed as he faced the skill of a man trained to live and die with the bladed weapons. Then he noticed that the Doctor was consistently moving more rapidly than Raul, forcing Raul to turn on his injured leg. While Raul was making frequent thrusts and passes at the Doctor, the Doctor rarely had to block them — he seemed to be moving one step ahead of his opponent. Then, unexpectedly, the Doctor went on the offensive, driving Raul around the floor. Within seconds, the Doctor gained the advantage. The Captain saw Raul fall, disarmed, with the Doctor's sword at his throat.

"Your life is forfeit to me and mine, Raul, and the innocence of my man is proved by your own laws."

"Then kill me quickly, in honor."

"In honor, I shall not do that. I would establish the truth of the matter — for all we have proved here is that I am a better swordsman than you. I will give you leave to probe the mind of my liege-man for the truth — if you will agree to verify it by putting your cousin Namona under the truth-spell."

"This is not in accordance with our ways."

"Is death then more important to you than truth?" Raul glared at the Doctor. The Doctor's sword remained steadily at his exposed throat.

"I will grant you what you ask."

A murmur rose up around the hall. The Doctor moved his sword to one side and Raul stood.

"Quiet. It will be as I have said. Call forth your man." Raul turned. "Summon Namona and El Donna."

"Captain," the Doctor motioned The Captain to the center of the floor. He unbuckled the scabbard and let the weapons fall to the floor. The Captain moved quickly.

As he handed the Doctor his coats, he whispered, "What's going to happen?"

"We'll let them find out what really happened." The Doctor shrugged into his longer outer coat, wrapped his scarf around his throat, and settled his hat on his head. "Raul will mind-probe you. Just concentrate on what happened. He isn't interested in anything else."

Namona, dressed all in white, eyes cast down, entered from the other side. With her was another woman, slighter, darker, with a ruby slipper worn in the hollow of her neck.

The two women joined the men in the center of the hall.

"El Donna," said Raul, "Place Namona under the truthspell."

"As you wish, Raul." The words were submissive but The Captain felt that had she so wished a refusal could as easily have been given. She turned to Namona. "Child, look at me." Namona's eyes raised and as they met the other's the slipper at El Donna's throat pulsed with energy. Namona stood, eyes fixed on space. El Donna turned back to Raul. "It is done."

Raul faced The Captain. The Captain looked down into the dark eyes and was suddenly thankful that the Doctor had been the one fighting this man.

The mind contact was sudden and sharp, quite unlike any feeling The Captain had ever had with The Scientist. This was a knife burning in his mind. For a moment The Captain tried to resist.

Then, remembering what the Doctor had said, he concentrated instead on the happening in the square.

The contact broke off. The Captain felt weakened and thankful that the Doctor had moved over and taken his arm.

Raul turned to the wide-eyed girl, "So, then, is this how it was?"

The Captain felt that he could almost see the exchange between the two minds.

"Yes, it is as he remembers."

Raul's hand flew forward and Namona reeled under the blow.

The Captain started toward Raul, but the Doctor restrained him.

"Fool!" Raul turned to El Donna. "See that she is returned to the nursery for another year until she is prepared to live with adults."

"As you wish." El Donna motioned and two women came and removed the now sobbing girl.

Raul faced the Doctor and ceremoniously bowed. "All honor to you and your liegeman. My home is yours."

"Honor to you for being willing to make a change." The Doctor replied, bowing in return. He stood for a moment, looking at Raul questioningly. "If you can accept change, then I would talk to you for a moment before we leave."

"Very well." Raul called toward the door. "Rad!" A young man stepped forward from the group on the far side. "See that horses and an escort are provided for our guests. El Donna, while the liegelord and I speak, will you accompany the liegeman to the horses?"

El Donna nodded her head in agreement.

Raul turned back to the Doctor, "No doubt your liegeman will wish to check that everything is in order."

"No doubt," replied the Doctor wryly, glancing at The Captain.

The Doctor and Raul walked off together. The Captain noticed that while his legs still seemed to be stable, the fog had returned, edging his thoughts.

"Captain?" It was El Donna. "Will you please come with me? We can await Raul and the Doctor outside."

She turned and led the way through the building. As they reached the entrance, The Captain was thankful to see that there were some stone benches in front. The horses and escort were not yet there.

"May we sit while we're waiting?" The Captain asked.

El Donna nodded. He was thankful that she did not seem disposed to chatter, yet he wanted to ask some questions.

"You have questions, Captain?"

"Yes. If it would not be offensive. I do not understand all of your ways."

"I think that you understand very few of our ways, but you may ask your questions."

With an effort, The Captain tried to concentrate on the main point. The fog seemed to clear for a minute; he noticed that the slipper at El Donna's neck was glowing. "Why did Raul hit Namona?" Gods, he thought, that was blunt.

"A blunt question is preferable if it enables the appropriate answer. Raul hit Namona for two reasons. First, it is customary among our women — especially those with high powers — not to look at any man other than one's own family until after marriage. You seem shocked, Captain, but I can tell you that her bold glances of themselves would have been sufficient to require punishment. As it was, her worst crime was in claiming forced violation after she read your response to her given invitation."

"You're saying she read my mind? What I was thinking about her?" The Captain felt a sudden sinking feeling — his thoughts?—a mental rape — and they said she was guilty?

"But I did...".

"Captain." The lithe figure turned to him and dark eyes gazed sympathetically but with some hint of amusement into his. "Have you ever physically raped a woman?"

"No." Never had to, he thought and felt himself flush as he saw by the answering gleam in her eyes that she had caught that additional thought.

"Our custom of not looking at strange men is for our own protection. There are some whose thoughts would be without doubt- -rape. Your thoughts, on the other hand — oh yes, Raul read them, so have we all — were flattering, stimulating and exciting, for any woman who was the direct object of them. You are embarrassed. There is no need to be. We all have our passions and desires, and yours for Namona was not in any way perverted or debased. Her reaction, on the other hand, showed that she does not yet deserve to be called woman, but is still a child, and will now be treated so. What she did could have caused at least one needless death, had it not been for your liege-lord. Can you understand this?"

It was strange but—"Yes. Although I must say that I will be thankful to leave this planet. I don't like the feeling that my mind is open to everyone."

"Not to everyone. That would be dishonorable, and exhausting, for the true telepath. I have just been scanning your surface thoughts because it seemed that it would facilitate our conversation."

There was a clatter of hooves, and The Captain saw the horses were being brought round. He wondered if he was going to be able to make it back. He felt the fog disappear and a soft strength enter his body. He turned to the woman beside him. Her eyes were closed and the jewel at her throat was pulsing. The dark eyes opened and looked into his, "You will make it back — and to your home." A gentle smile seemed to caress him. "I must go now. Raul and the Doctor are coming."

The Captain eyed the horses without enthusiasm. While he was feeling better, he was not a horseman. Somehow the thought of subjecting his still sore muscles to another trip on the beast was not appealing. Beside him he heard El Donna sigh. "This much too, then, Captain." He looked back down at her to see the slipper pulsing again.

"What?"

"It is a small thing, Captain. A gift from me to you. That you may have some not-so-unpleasant memories of this planet." The Doctor and Raul were coming out of the door. She turned and left.

"Coming, Captain?" said the Doctor as he moved past The Captain and mounted the horse.

The Captain followed, getting on the horse behind the Doctor's. As he mounted, he realized that somehow his body seemed to know how to ride and handle the animal. Things fit — the double reins, the saddle and stirrups — he was part of the animal. The Captain looked over to the doorway where El Donna was standing. An enigmatic smile was on her lips as the group rode away.

Riding through the hills he thought about her. The Doctor had pulled slightly ahead and was talking to the leader of their escorts, the young man Raul had called Rad.

Why was the armed escort needed, The Captain wondered. There had been no trouble on the way up and the countryside certainly seemed peaceful. Now, at mid-morning, there was not even the need for the leather jacket he had worn on the ride up.

A brilliant flash of light and shouting broke his thoughts. Lasers? The leading members of the party and their mounts had gone down. The Doctor was reining his horse sharply around. Without hesitation, The Captain followed.

"Rad," the Doctor called, "Get out of here!"

"We do not retreat!" The young man answered. The Captain saw that the remaining party were pulling out their swords, preparing to attack.

Swords against lasers? The Captain kicked his horse into a gallop and headed down the trail after the Doctor. The light flared again and the Doctor looked back. He shook has head and led the way off the trail into a rocky pass.

"Let the horses go. They'll be good decoys." The Doctor dismounted and gave his horse a slap on the rump, sending it on its way. The Captain quickly followed suit. As his horse galloped away, he followed the Doctor up the side of the mountain and jointed him, crouching behind a large rock.

"What was that all about?"

"Tin Woodmen," said the Doctor grimly.

"Who are the Tin Woodmen?"

"The ones who invaded this planet before. Apparently they left a small group behind to keep the pressure on as the bombs came down." The Doctor cautiously stood up and looked over the top of the rock. The Captain stayed down, watching him.

"You are the Doctor." A metallic artificial voice echoes from the rocks. The Doctor stood completely still, motioning The Captain to stay down.

"Dissect the Doctor!"

"No. I wish to question him first."

At least two of them out there, The Captain thought. Probably more. There was an utterly vicious quality to the voices. The Doctor was moving around to the front of the rock. No time for plans or signals. Did the Doctor expect him to follow and attempt a rescue or leave?

"Put that down," said a metallic voice and a brief flare of light flickered among the rocks.

"It's only a toy," said the Doctor plaintively.

"You will come with us. You will keep your hands in sight. Now."

"Well, there's no need to shove."

The Captain heard noises as the group moved away. He peered cautiously around one corner of the rock. He could see the Doctor and four strange dome-shaped metal creatures about five feet high moving down the path. He waited until they went around a bend and started to follow.

As he came out, he saw a mark on one of the rocks and, looking down, saw a yo-yo on the ground. He picked it up. A child's toy, but the Doctor had risked something to leave it. If the Doctor had done that, then there might be a purpose for it.

He continued to trail the Doctor and his captors. Some type of a robot — but with an independent mind, The Captain thought. Certainly an eminently practical design, not at all anthropomorphic. The weaponry they used seemed to be built-in as one of the projections from the center of the bulletlike body. The other projection was probably a 'hand', although it bore no resemblance to anything humanoid. A third projection near the round-

ed top rotated as if the creature used it as an eye.
He could not tell how they were moving. The base
of the body was so close to the ground that nothing could be seen. No wheels in this terrain —
maybe some type of an air suspension system?
However they had come about, their creation was
inspired and, with the attitude they seemed to
have, diabolical.

The group came to a circular stone structure.
After a brief noise, an opening appeared in one
side of the structure. The opening closed as soon
as they went in. Some kind of forcefield, The Captain decided. He crept cautiously up to the sides.
Solid rock, but the structure stopped about nine
feet up. Where there's a wall, there's a way, The
Captain thought. The fog began pressing on his
mind again but he fought it, finally succeeding in
pushing it back. These Tin Woodmen did not have
feet or legs or real arms, so they might not be prepared for someone attacking from the top of the
wall. He found hand and footholds in the rough
rock and got to the top. He realized that he had
carried the yo-yo in his mouth, like a weapon.
Could it become one?, he wondered.

Lying down flat on top, he looked down inside.
The Doctor stood in the middle of the structure. A
strange light surrounded him.

"Why have you come here?" asked one of the
Tin Woodmen and the light around the Doctor
changed color. The Doctor did not respond and
the light flickered again. It seemed to be tighten-
ing on him. Another force field, The Captain decided.

"I was just looking around. What are you doing
here?" The Doctor lifted his head and smiled at
the nearest Tin Woodman.

At least he was conscious, and if he was conscious, and if the forcefield could be removed...The Captain moved slowly along the wall looking for some type of control panel inside the complex.

"Insufficient," intoned the metallic voice, "You will tell the truth."

"Exterminate!" another Tin Woodman demanded.

"No. He may have information we need."

The light changed color again and The Captain heard the Doctor gasp. If he didn't act quickly, the Doctor would not be able to escape. The Captain spotted what looked like a control panel — switches, buttons and flashing lights. He crawled so that he was directly above it. Now — one leap down. He glanced over at the Doctor to catch a definite glance that said 'no'.

"Do you still like blue?" the Doctor casually asked his Tin Woodman inquisitor.

"That is not an answer." The light changed again.

Blue? There was one panel glowing that color. The Captain looked at the Doctor and then at the yo-yo in his hand. He lifted it. Heavy — maybe not just a normal yo-yo then. And on a string. The Captain smiled at it. Method in the Doctor's madness. He tied one end of the string to his finger and sent the weight down toward the panel. Missed. He pulled it back up and tried again.

"You will tell us what we wish to know."

"Difficult without breathing."

The Captain felt the weight rebound as the yo-yo hit the panel and broke it. The power over the complex died. The Doctor ran for the opening. The Captain slid off the wall just as the Doctor ran around to meet him. The Doctor pulled him

The Doctor and the Enterprise

down behind another rock. "Stay here. They'll be expecting us to run."

They remained hidden until dusk came, saying nothing. The Doctor motioned and The Captain followed him up further into the mountains. A small cave seemed to be an acceptable stopping place and the Doctor motioned The Captain inside. The Captain collapsed on one side and looked at the Doctor who was leaning against the other wall.

"Doctor," said The Captain, "Don't you know any nice people?"

The Doctor turned to The Captain, "Where did you learn to ride like that in one day?"

The Captain looked at him suddenly at a loss. Oh no, he thought, he's off on a tangent. Still, the blue eyes looking into his were quite serious.

"I think that El Donna did something to me before we left."

"Physically?"

"I think so. I feel better and I did know how to handle that horse. I can't think of any other way for that to have happened."

"That last bit of riding probably saved your life. And now..."

The Captain waited patiently. The Doctor seemed to be in another world. The Captain now realized this was part of the way the alien mind worked. They were alone in a wilderness with no weapons or communication devices, pursued by Tin Woodmen. Anything the Doctor could think of would help.

"Do you have any psychic abilities?" the Doctor asked.

"No. I've always tested negative."

"Tests aren't always the whole answer."

"What are you thinking of doing?"

"There is one possibility." The Doctor stopped

and looked down at his hands. The Captain realized that one of them had been burned by the Tin
Woodman's weapon.

"If there is any possibility, I'm willing to try it.
What do you want me to do?"

The Doctor studied The Captain carefully as he
spoke. "El Donna is the most powerful psychic on
this planet. You have recently been in telepathic
contact with her. For her to do what she did, she
obviously felt some attraction to you." He
stopped.

The Captain waited and when the Doctor did
not continue said, "The problem is that I'm not a
telepath, so I can't reach her. Can't you reach
her?"

"I haven't had the contact I need to establish a
link. I know of her — I don't know her." The
Doctor seemed to be studying the side of the rock.

"Doctor, if you will tell me what you want me
to do, I will do it." The Doctor looked at The Captain and smiled.

"What I want you to do is to try to reach El
Donna mentally. I will tap into your mind, enable
your signal — boost it, and then talk to her
through your mind."

"You want me to be a link between the two of
you?"

"A signal and a link. It will not be easy."

The Captain examined the Doctor intently, finally deciding he was serious. "Let's try it then.
What do I do?"

"Picture her in your mind. As clearly and accu-
rately as you can. When the picture is sharp, call
her name."

The Captain nodded and leaned back against
the wall and closed his eyes. He felt one of the
Doctor's hands resting lightly on his head. Odd,

he thought, he could easily accept the idea of telepathy through touch, but over a distance...

It can be done.

The Doctor's thought in his mind was as unique as his voice. Not like The Scientist at all.

Mind-touch is a matchless means of identification. Think of El Donna.

Obediently, The Captain tried to remember her. The dark eyes, the smile, the tilt of her head, the mass of dark green hair, the image swirled in his mind but he could not seem to stabilize it. He realized that he was breathing more rapidly and the Doctor's hand dropped away. He opened his eyes and looked at the Doctor. The Doctor was looking at the opposite wall of the cave. He seemed almost discouraged. Damn, The Captain thought, we can't give up now.

"Try again?" he said lightly.

"Do you feel up to it? This may turn out to be physically painful to you, and in your present condition...".

"I'll make it."

The Doctor studied him for a moment, almost as if he recognized The Captain's tone of voice. Maybe he did from his contact with The Scientist. It was The Captain at his best, in command and not to be trifled with.

The Captain closed his eyes again, waiting for the Doctor's hand to come back to his face. When contact was established The Captain summoned the image again. It came, moving, refusing to become firm. He felt weak. No wonder The Scientist was leery of using the mind-meld if it was as tiring as this. Come on, he thought, when have you ever had trouble remembering a pretty face?

Something is missing. The Doctor thought. Missing?

The Captain tried not to look at the image but to think about the woman he had just left.

The slipper. He thought at the Doctor.

Of course, the slipper is part of her.

The Captain grabbed the floating image and placed the ruby slipper at her neck. Immediately the image became sharp and clear. As if she was in his mind, looking at him. He felt the Doctor's mind move in his.

Now — call her!

El Donna...El Donna!

Without warning, another mind touched his. He felt his body double over in spasms. The Doctor's other hand caught and cradled his head.

Captain? Why are you calling me?

The spasm seemed to ease slightly as he felt her mind settle into his.

The Doctor needs to talk to you.

The Doctor? Your liegelord?

Yes. Here...

The Captain felt the Doctor's mind move forward and meet El Donna's. Now he could sit back and let these two handle it.

The invaders—the Tin Woodmen—are still here. A rear guard, in the mountains.

So the machines have not gone.

They have killed our escort. We must join now to destroy them.

Before myself and others of the greatest power joined with the machine lovers—those whom you call the Techies. Now the others of the Power who joined with me are gone. Our powers are diminished. Our weapons cannot equal theirs. What can we do??

It is possible that an avalanche could be triggered on their camp. Do you have enough of the Power left to do that?

I would need the assistance of others. They will have to come from afar. It will take time.

The Captain felt himself being stirred from his bystander role.

Doctor. He could sense that his body was objecting to the effort it was taking to enter the conversation.

What?

You are not alone in this.

What do you mean?

There is the Enterprise.

The Doctor did not respond.

Had you forgotten?

What about your Directive?

To Hell with the Directive!

He could feel the Doctor's laughter and it somehow made the pain in his body ease. Captain, I think I like you.

Can we reach her?

Who is this Enterprise? El Donna questioned sharply.

It is his ship.

Strange—to love a machine so.

Doctor. The Captain realized that if they did not act quickly his body would collapse from the effects of the linking. Can we reach The Scientist?

Image him for me, Captain, and I shall reach him. El Donna's mental voice was brisk and quite matter-of-fact.

The Captain again tried to summon a mental image...this time, The Scientist. He felt his muscles quivering as if he had been running too long.

With this image I can help. The Doctor's mind swept into his.

The image he had been striving for sharpened, became clear.

Captain, I can drop you from the link now.

No Doctor. This time he was the one laughing. If you want the Enterprise to fire her lasers on this planet, I have to give the order.

If it costs your life?

If it does—then it does. He felt his muscles contract again.

Captain...as you wish it.

One part of his mind seemed to feel the Doctor holding him, the other brought the image of The Scientist into focus again.

El Donna. The Doctor called. The image—can you reach this man?

Yes.

And The Scientist was there.

Captain?! The Scientist's mind seemed reassuringly familiar.

Scientist. Full lasers...El Donna's mind was there, linked with the Doctor's and coordinates appeared in his mind.

Captain—the Directive?

Scientist—No good to give The Scientist the answer that had so readily satisfied the Doctor. The Tin Woodmen, the ones who invaded this planet before—still here—they're the violators. He felt his body spasm violently again and knew that the three minds in his felt it too.

Captain? Doctor, get him out of this!

My decision, Scientist. You have your orders.

And the world slid away.

When he came to, The Captain found himself lying on the cave floor wrapped in the Doctor's coat. The Doctor was standing at the entrance looking out.

"Doctor?" He tried to lift his head.

The Doctor moved back and made him lie down.

"Don't try to move. You won't have the strength. Don't even try to talk. The Scientist will never forgive me if I don't get you back safely."

The Captain took a deep breath. The Doctor was right. He didn't have any strength left.

"You missed the fireworks. That's the easiest time I've ever had with Tin Woodmen."

Odd, The Captain thought, he would have thought that the Doctor would be exuberant, but he seemed strangely subdued. He was taking a metal object out of his pocket—the sonic screwdriver The Engineer had been trying to analyze.

"I'm setting this to a signal your teleporter will be able to home in on. We should be having company soon." He smiled at The Captain as a small section of the screwdriver seemed to extend. "At least you won't have to ride a horse back."

THE FREDDY KRUEGER STORY

The making of the monster. Including interviews with director Wes Craven and star Robert Englund. Plus an interview with Freddy himself! $14.95

THE ALIENS STORY

Interviews with movie director James Cameron, stars Sigourney Weaver and Michael Biehn and effects people and designers Ron Cobb, Syd Mead, Doug Beswick and lots more!...$14.95

ROBOCOP

Law enforcement in the future. Includes interviews with the stars, the director, the writer, the special effects people, the storyboard artists and the makeup men! $16.95

MONSTERLAND'S HORROR IN THE '80s

The definitive book of the horror films of the '80s. Includes interviews with the stars and makers of Aliens, Freddy Krueger, Robocop, Predator, Fright Night, Terminator and all the others! $17.95

LOST IN SPACE

THE COMPLEAT LOST IN SPACE
244 PAGES...$17.95
TRIBUTE BOOK
Interviews with everyone!...$7.95
TECH MANUAL
Technical diagrams to all of the special ships and devices plus exclusive production artwork....$9.95

GERRY ANDERSON

SUPERMARIONATION
Episode guides and character profiles to Capt Scarlet, Stingray, Fireball, Thunderbirds, Supercar and more...240 pages...$17.95

BEAUTY AND THE BEAST

THE UNOFFICIAL BEAUTY&BEAST
Complete first season guide including interviews and biographies of the stars. 132 pages $14.95

DARK SHADOWS

DARK SHADOWS TRIBUTE BOOK
Interviews, scripts and more... 160 pages...$14.95

DARK SHADOWS INTERVIEWS BOOK
A special book interviewing the entire cast. $18.95

DOCTOR WHO THE BAKER YEARS

A complete guide to Tom Baker's seasons as the Doctor including an in-depth episode guide, interviews with the companions and profiles of the characters... 0 pages...$19.95

THE DOCTOR WHO ENCYCLOPEDIA: THE FOURTH DOCTOR

Encyclopedia of every character, villain and monster of the Baker Years. ..240 pages...$19.95